Blades . . . vs. Black Magic

Cyron, the dark-bearded pirate, clutching sword and shield, leaped to the low rail, his voice lifted in a battle cry. He stood petrified. Upon the lofty after cabin there had suddenly appeared a swarthy Minoan priest. Above the uproar of battle, his voice lifted in a wailing chant.

"O great Minos, whose years are twenty generations, who is god of all the world! O great Cybele, mother of Earth and Minos and Men! O great Dark One, whose name may not be uttered! O great gods of Knossos, destroy these vermin— strike!"

The black priest held high the red-dripping vessel, and down from the silver horns leaped a shaft of blue fire. Thunder crashed deafeningly. And Cyron, sword and shield slipping from his limp hands, dropped loose-limbed to the deck.

The Reign of Wizardry is a gem of fantasy from the golden age of the supreme magazine of the imagination, *Unknown*. It has never before appeared in book form.

COMPLETE AND UNABRIDGED

THE
REIGN
OF
WIZARDRY

Jack Williamson

LANCER BOOKS • NEW YORK

A LANCER BOOK • 1964

THE REIGN OF WIZARDRY—by Jack Williamson

LANCER BOOKS, INC. • 26 WEST 47TH STREET • NEW YORK 36, N.Y.

Foreword

ONCE THERE was an island empire. Its fleets ruled the seas for a thousand years. Its wealth and splendor dazzled all the world. Then it was destroyed—cataclysmically!

Its fall still presents a mystery. For it was cut off abruptly, in the full tide of power. The fleets that had guarded its rich commerce and its unwalled cities were suddenly no more. Its capital city, where men had dwelt for ten thousand years, was looted and burned and leveled by earthquake shock. Its people were scattered, and presently lost even the memory of their departed greatness.

The history of that empire's splendor and its passing became a legend. Generations of retelling confused the details. Men came to call that lost world Atlantis, and at last began to doubt that it had ever been.

But the account of Atlantis that Plato heard from the Egyptian priests—in almost every detail save the vague location beyond the Pillars of Hercules, and the complete submersion of the land itself—fits what is now known of Minoan Crete.

The conquerors, also, told their own story of what happened. Minos the god-king, the monstrous Minotaur of the Labyrinth, the artificer Daedalus, fair-tressed Ariadne and the victorious Greek hero, all became the figures of a splendid myth.

But merely a myth—until, a hundred years ago, a poor child named Heinrich Schlieman was given a storybook of Homeric Greece. He saw a picture of the walls of Troy, and said that such walls could not have been obliterated, even in three thousand years.

Schlieman ignored the derision of scholars. Beginning life as an ill-paid grocer's clerk, he educated himself, made a fortune, and at last realized his splendid, stubborn dream—he excavated the mound at Hissarlik, and found not one Troy, but nine!

The forgotten gates of a magnificent pre-Homeric world were thus thrown open to knowledge. Sir Arthur Evans was one of the brilliant men who followed Schlieman. He uncovered the great building that was the very heart of that lost world—the Palace of Minos at Knossos in Crete.

Even the carved stone throne of Minos has been preserved, with the griffin frescoes that graced the throne room; a cast of it may be seen in New York's Metropolitan Museum. Excavations at other sites in Crete, at Mycenae and Tiryns, have filled out the picture of a reality more amazing than the legend of Atlantis and the myths of the Greeks.

It was a strangely modern world, whose remains the spades have brought to light. Uncannily modern, in matters as various as plumbing and art and architecture and women's gowns. Every find at Knossos helps bring to life a gay and sophisticated court.

But the Minoan world had its darker side. Archæology supports the grim legend of the Minotaur. Wall paintings show men and girls engaged in the deadly game of "bull vaulting"; and Dr. Evans found even the dungeon pits, in which the victims of a cruel religion must have awaited sacrifice.

After all the scraps of knowledge have been pieced together, however, Minoan Crete remains a strange and fascinating riddle. The Minoans, it is true, left records. They were, in fact, the first printers—on clay—from movable type; and the alphabet itself may have been carried from them to the Phoenicians after the disaster by the Philistines, who seem to have been Minoan émigrés. The Minoan script known a "Linear B" was brilliantly deciphered in the early 1950's by Michael Ventris, turning out to be Greek. Other recent work in Minoan archæology has generated more controversy than fact, however; and the true history of the fall of Knossos is still veiled in myth and magic.

The fall of the ruthless and decadent Minoan despotism, it seems, must have been one of the decisive events of history. For the democracy and the civilization of Greece, the basis of our own, could have been built only upon the ruins of the Minoan age. The Greek conqueror, then, is one of the supreme men of history. Legend has brought us his name— Theseus.

Knossos fell. The coincidence of earthquake and sword and torch is still a riddle. But the world's oldest and greatest palace was turned into a mound of ruin. For three thousand years it lay abandoned, "uncanny, haunted ground."

Magic and ritual—as the findings of Evans and McKenzie and Pendlebury and the Haweses and others confirm—played a grimly dominant part in the life of Crete. Immemorial Knossos may well have been the cradle of the magical arts. The jigsaw puzzle of myth and archæology and the fragmentary Egyptian records seem inevitably to fall into a dreadful pattern. The most plausible answer to all the riddles of Minoan Crete is—wizardry!

ONE

"WHAT ARE the omens, Captain Firebrand?" Cyron, the bearded Dorian pirate, looked nervous. A hairy hand clutched one of the stays that supported the long galley's single mast, and his scarred face was apprehensive as he peered across the glancing blue water between the green headlands. "Shall we run for the islands?"

Theseus, the tall Achean, stood near the high wolf's-head standard that rose above the prow. His legs were set wide against the roll and toss of the narrow ship, and his long red hair whipped back in the wind. He shaded his blue eyes, and looked with Cyron into the strait ahead.

Dancing on the white-glinting blue, between the points of land, he found two black dots and a yellow one. He studied them carefully, and the cloud-streaked westward sky, and the ruffled track of the wind upon the sea.

At last his hard tanned body straightened, in the simple loincloth of captured Egyptian linen. He tossed his red mane back again, and his quick voice rang above the weary monotonous chant of the oar slaves and the creak of the wind-strained rigging.

"The wind is with us, Gamecock," he said. "They are only two against our one—we can forget the trader until the war galleys are sunk. And our bronze beak makes us the equal of three—you said so yourself, when we rammed the last Egyptian."

"Yes, Captain Fireband," agreed the anxious Dorian. "But *that* was an Egyptian—"

The hairy pirate shuddered a little, in the long stiff cloak of bead-embroidered purple silk that had belonged to a Cretan naval officer. But Theseus drew the long straight sword from his belt, and looked into the polish of its blue steel.

"The men are hungry for plunder," he told Cyron. "And the Falling Star is thirsty for blood." A tense little smile touched his lean face. "I read my omens in the mirror of the Falling Star," he said, "and they are always good!"

He turned on the planking that decked the narrow bow, and shouted past the mast to the slave-driver perched on the lip of the oarsmen's pit beyond:

"A faster stroke! We must cut them off before they pass the headland!"

"Aye, Captain Firebrand!"

The Mycenean's long whip hissed and cracked. Forty-four slaves bent to twenty-two oars, eleven to the side. Their endless chant grew swifter, and the galley leapt to its rhythm.

"Hail, Captain Firebrand!" came a shout from the two score of sailors and fighting men crowded on the deck above the after cabin, beyond the pit. "Do we fight again?"

Theseus cupped tanned hands to his face. "We fight," he shouted. "And when the lots are cast, we shall have treasure from the north coasts to divide. Gold and amber and furs— and perhaps even fair northern slaves!"

Cheers answered, and he ordered:

"All hands make ready to attack and board!"

Bronze blades rang to the stone. Archers flexed and strung their bows, a slinger stretched his thongs. The boarding crew fitted on leathern helmets, laid ready their long bullhide shields. At his fire above the pit, the one-eyed Tirynthian cook began heating pots of sulphur.

But Cyron shook his scarred dark head uneasily. Anxiously fingering the edges of the beaded cape, he stepped close to Theseus and protested in a husky whisper:

"But those leading sails are black, Captain Firebrand."

"I see that they are black, Gamecock."

"The black sails mean that they are war galleys of the royal navy of Minos," rasped the apprehensive pirate. "They are guarded by the uncanny artifices of the warlock Daedalus, and by the wizardry of Minos himself. There will be black priests of the Dark One aboard them, to blast our bodies and our souls with their deadly magic."

Urgently, he touched the bronze arm of Theseus. "Let us turn and run for the islands, Captain Firebrand," he begged, "before their tricks of wizardry set the wind against us, to shatter us against some hostile coast!

"Let us wait for an Egyptian galley," he pleaded huskily, "guarded only by the distant sleepy gods of the Nile. Or perhaps a trader from the East, that trusts in the dusty deities of dead Babylon. Or maybe we shall meet another merchant that carries only the feeble godlings of Troy."

10

His hairy hand trembled. "Captain Firebrand, we dare not defy the gods and the warlocks of Crete—your attacks must already have angered them, and their wizardry is the strongest in the world. An Egyptian priest told me once—before I disemboweled him—that all magic came first from that evil island. Shall we turn back, Captain?"

Theseus touched the gleaming gold-and-silver inlay that covered the hilt of the Falling Star.

"Not so long as I am your elected captain, Gamecock," he said soberly. "I joined your ship, a year ago, because the pirates are the only men in the world who defy the magic and the fleets of Crete. Even the great Pharaoh flatters Minos, and sends him gifts of silver and black slaves and apes."

Cyron looked up at the taller, clean-shaven Achean, with a look of uneasy admiration.

"I know you have done mighty deeds, Captain Firebrand," he said, "for the stories follow you. I know that you have destroyed savage animals, and slain outlaws and tyrants, and fought the men of far lands. But aren't your deeds great enough to rest upon? Must you make war against the wizards, and earn the anger of the very gods?"

The red head of Theseus nodded slowly, and his face was very grave. "I must," he said. "For always I have fought the enemies of men. And the greatest enemy is not the man-hunting animals, nor outlaws, nor barbarian tribes. It is not lurking in the wilderness, but it rules in the heart of the greatest city!"

His hard fingers drew the steel half out of its scabbard. "The greatest enemy is magic, Gamecock. It is the wizardry of Crete that enslaves the world. Even in the tents of the desert, men cower in fear before a talisman that bears the double ax of Minos." His tense face had turned a little white. "All nations send a tribute of boys and girls to be trained for the cruel games at Knossos. Even my own Attica is subject to Minos—my own father, at Athens, must kneel to the Cretan resident, and send gifts to the Dark One."

His breath made a sharp angry sound. "The wizardry of Knossos is a dark serpent that coils about the spirits of men," he said bitterly. "The cruel sea-power of Minos is enforced with fear of the Dark One."

The sword flashed clear of the scabbard. "Well, Gamecock —Minos and the Dark One must be destroyed!"

Cyron clutched the bronzed sword arm, desperately.

"Hush, captain!" he gasped apprehensively. "That is blasphemy—and the ears and the horns of the Dark One are long!" He caught his breath. "You musunderstand us, Captain Firebrand. It is true that we are pirates, true that piracy is against the law of Minos. But, until you joined us, we had preyed only upon the shipping of Egypt and Tiryns and suchlike rivals of Crete—so that the captains of Minos winked at us."

"But now," Theseus reminded him, "I am your elected captain."

"And a good one—if you would forget this madness of a one-man war against the wizardy of Crete," Cyron yielded. "This bronze beak you built upon the galley has already sunk a dozen ships for us."

Grimly, Theseus shook his head. "I invented the ram to destroy the power of Minos," he said slowly. "But, alone, it isn't enough. Great Ekoros, they say, and even the palace of Knossos itself, have no defensive walls. But that Cretan priest boasted to me—before I cut his lying throat—that the power of Minos is guarded by three walls.

"First there is the fleet, that they call the wooden wall. And then, the priest said, there is a giant of living brass, named Talos—he is the second wall."

Cyron plucked uncomfortably at his beard. "I have heard of Talos," he agreed apprehensively. "He is twice the height of a man, and so fleet of foot that he runs around all Crete in a day. He crushes his enemies in his arms, and roasts them against the hot metal of his body. I shall never touch that isle of evil!"

"Unless the Cretans take you there, to feed their Dark One!" Theseus grinned at him. "Then there is another barrier about the power of Minos, that is called the third wall." He stared at the far black sails. "The ram will break the wooden wall, perhaps. But there are still two more to pass."

Cyron pulled the purple cloak defensively about him. "All the walls of Crete," he declared, "are better left alone!"

"We shall see." Theseus smiled again, and a tanned thumb tried his sword. "You had better find your spurs, Gamecock. The Cretans are turning to meet us!"

Theseus walked aft, giving orders and grinning encouragement to the archers climbing to the foredeck, the boarding party waiting with their grapnels in the waist, the slingers on the cabin, the one-eyed cook, Vorkos, coughing over his pots of boiling sulphur. He felt the sharp unease that chilled them all, like a freezing wind.

"Ready, men!" he shouted. "Are you afraid of an old man's muttering? There is a magic in hot blood and good bronze that is stronger than all the wizardry of Minos. Our beak would sink the galley of Admiral Phaistro himself." He flourished his sword in a glittering circle. "And the Falling Star has an enchantment stronger than the Dark One. It was hammered from metal that fell from heaven. You have seen it sever blades of bronze. If you fear the wizards, you are already conquered. If you don't, their power can't touch you! Now, will you follow me?"

He waited, concealing his anxiety.

"Aye, Captain Firebrand!" The shout rang from half a hundred throats. "We will follow you!"

But he heard the doubt, the dread, that lingered in it. He knew that these pirates, boldest men as they were of a dozen northern coasts, still shared Cyron's awe of the wizardry of Crete. They would follow—but not all the way.

It came to Theseus that he stood all alone against the gods of Crete. And even in his own heart was a small, cold fear. For he had met magicians, and he knew that they possessed undeniable powers.

He was glad when the ships came into fighting range. Singing a bold song, the sailors quickly lowered the square red sheet, unshipped the mast. The first flight of arrows flashed out from the Cretan archers, and fell short in the water.

The Mycenean cursed, and his black whip cracked, and red sweat ran down the backs of the slaves in their pit. Theseus called brief orders to Gothung, the tall blond steersman. And the pirate galley swept in toward the Cretans.

The Cretan officers followed conventional tactics. They raced down upon the quarters of the pirate. Then, at the last moment, their slave shipped the exposed banks of oars.

The object of the maneuver was to bring the ships together in a glancing collision, shearing off unshipped oars and crushing the enemy's rowers with their shattering ends, and then grapple for boarding.

But Theseus snapped quick orders to the Mycenean slave-

13

driver and the gigantic Northman at the steering oars. The pirate swept aside from the path of the racing Cretans, and came about in a swift, puzzling curve.

The two Cretans, briefly helpless with oars shipped, crashed together. Before their slaves, screaming to the whips, could thrust them apart, the pirate drove with flashing oars against the side of the nearest. The bronze ram ripped through the planking, below the waterline.

The Cretan archers loosed a storm of arrows. Slung stones hummed, burning sulphur made a suffocating reek. A gang of Cretan marines flung grapnel hooks, then crouched waiting with their nets and tridents to swarm aboard.

But their roof of shields protected the pirates on the narrow bow. Axes severed the grapnel lines, and straining slaves backed the galley.

The bronze beak retreated, and water poured into the Cretan galley. It listed sluggishly, a wave poured over the heavy prow, and it went down with chained slaves shrieking at the oars. Armor-laden men struggled briefly in the foaming sea.

The other Cretan, meantime, had dipped her oars again. Before the pirate could move forward once more, the two long galleys veered together. Theseus shouted an order for the slaves on the exposed side to draw in their oars.

The hulls crashed. Grapnels caught and ropes whipped tight. Bows twanged and slung stones drummed on shields. Smoke of sulphur and cordage and human flesh made a choking stench.

"Board them!" shouted Theseus. "Sixty shekels of silver to the first man over the rail!"

"Aye, Captain Firebrand!"

Cyron, the dark-bearded Dorian, clutching sword and shield, leaped to the low rail of the pirate. For an instant he stood there, his voice lifted in a battle cry. Then abruptly the cry was cut short. He stood petrified.

Upon the lofty after cabin of the Cretan, there had suddenly appeared a swarthy Minoan priest, wrapped in a long black sacerdotal robe. Above the uproar of the battle, his voice lifted in a wailing chant.

At first he used the secret priestly tongue, while his thin hands lifted a silver vessel that was shaped like a bull's head, and poured its foaming red contents into the sea. Then he changed to the common Cretan language, that Theseus had learned long ago from the traders who came to Athens.

14

"O great Minos," he wailed, "whose years are twenty generations, who is god of all the world! O great Cybele, mother of Earth and Minos and Men, whose dwelling is the most beauteous Ariadne! O great Dark One, whose name may not be uttered, who art bull and man and god! O great gods of Knossos, destroy these vermin who molest your faithful slaves!

"Bright sword of Minos, strike!"

The black priest held high the red-dripping vessel. And down from the silver horns leaped a blade of blue fire. Thunder crashed deafeningly. And Cyron, sword and shield slipping from his limp hands, dropped loose-limbed back to the pirate's deck.

Two

THE WHOLE battle had halted, to await the climax of the black priest's invocation. That strange bolt broke a breathless hush, and then Theseus heard the triumphant shout of the Cretans. He heard the groan of anguish and terror that ran among the pirates, saw them falter before the swift massing of the Cretan marines. He caught his breath, and lifted the bright steel sword.

"Follow me!" he shouted. "Follow the Falling Star—and stop the cowardly wizardry of Minos!"

He flung aside his heavy 8-shaped shield, too heavy for swift action. Bronze body stripped to the loins, he raced across the narrow deck. A hissing arrow brushed his hair, and a stone stung his arm. The bright sword deflected another arrow, and he leaped from the deck.

His feet spurned the rail. He leaped again from the roof of shields that covered a squad of crouching lancers, and stood upon the high cabin's roof. His naked sword menaced the black Minoan priest, and his voice pealed out: "Where now is the magic of Minos?"

He watched savage elation turn to terror in the smoky eyes of the priest. He saw the dark flash of cunning in them, and glimpsed thin hands pressing quickly on the eyes of the bull's head vessel.

His sword flashed. He heard a crackling sound, and saw a flash of blue, and caught a stinging odor. But the red-dripping silver vessel pitched out of dying hands into the sea. Severed clean, the priest's head followed it.

"Come!" shouted Theseus. "Follow the Falling Star!"

He leaped down from the cabin, in the rear of the Cretan boarders. His steel parried an arrow, and cleft the archer's throat. He snatched a bullhide shield from a dying lancer, and his sword slipped hilt-deep through another.

"Come on!" his deep voice pealed. "For the priest of the Dark One is dead!"

Under the eye of the limping Tirynthian cook, four men hurled a pot of blazing sulphur from a net. It spread blue choking flame. The Cretans stumbled back, some of them shrieking in agony. And the pirates swarmed after them, drove them against the busy sword of Theseus.

The galley was taken—but briefly, for the unquenchable sulphur flames swiftly recaptured it. The pirates retreated from the asphyxiating blaze, with such weapons and other loot as they could snatch. Theseus ordered the galley rammed, to end the screaming agony of the chained slaves, and then turned to pursue the yellow-sailed trader.

Now, after the battle was ended, he had a sudden sick awareness of the small margin by which death had passed him by. His arm was bleeding where the stone had stung him, and he found a long red mark across his ribs, where some point had thrust.

And the Falling Star trembled in his hands, as he had time to recall the strange bolt that had struck down Cyron. Uneasily he remembered the rumors that Minos ruled the lightning. His own dread of the wizardry of Knossos was not all conquered.

"Poor old Gamecock!" he whispered. "Perhaps you were right. Perhaps a man cannot defy the gods."

He dropped on his knees beside the bearded Dorian. He saw the tiny smoke that lifted from a smoldering spot on the stiff splendor of Cyron's beaded cloak; traced the long red burn, branching like a tree, that scarred the pirate's sword arm.

"The warlocks have a power," he muttered. "But you will be avenged, Gamecock." His lean jaw was hard. "Because I'm going on until I die—or until the gods of Crete have fallen!"

"Stay, Captain Firebrand!" Cyron gulped a long breath and opened his eyes. He sat up weakly on the deck, and his trembling fingers clutched desperately at the arm of Theseus. But Theseus was staring at his eyes. They were filmed and distended with horror.

"Forget your mad ambition, Captain Firebrand!" begged the choked dry voice of Cyron. "For I have felt the magic of Minos, and now I know the power of the Dark One—and it is a terrible power!"

"I know that it is terrible," Theseus told him gravely. "That is the reason that it must be destroyed." He grinned, and lifted Cyron to his feet. "You're a tough one, Gamecock! I thought you were dead."

"Almost," whispered the pirate, "I wish I were!"

The trader was a broad ship, deeply burdened, with but seven oars on the side to aid her huge square sail. The pirate, with red sail set again and oars dipping briskly, swiftly overhauled her.

A flight of arrows winged toward the pirate. But the trader carried no more than a score of freemen, to handle arms and sail. When Theseus promised to set them all alive upon the nearest land, her captain surrendered.

"A strange name you have made, Captain Firebrand!" commented Cyron. "There was never another pirate in these waters whose word would take a ship!"

"It isn't men I hate," Theseus told him. "It is the warlocks and gods of evil. We will set the captain and his men ashore on the headland, and leave them food and arms."

"A strange pirate, indeed!" Cyron grunted.

As the yellow sail had indicated, the trader belonged to the merchant fleet of Amur the Hittite, whose house had become great under the protection of Minos. Her captain was a hawk-nosed, sallow-cheeked nephew of Amur himself. It seemed to Theseus that he had accepted capture with a curious and almost alarming indifference.

The trader proved a rich prize. It was laden with gold and tin from the mines on the far northern rivers, and amber and hides and furs. In a narrow pen on the foredeck were three huge wild bulls from the plains of Thessaly. And lying fettered in the cabins were twelve strong youths and twelve tall, graceful girls, all blond-haired people of the north.

17

Besides the slave girls, there was another woman found unfettered in the Hittite captain's cabin—such a woman as none of the pirates had ever seen. Her skin was the color of gold, her dark smoldering eyes almond-shaped and queerly slanted.

She was dragged out upon the deck with the rest, to await her lot in the partition of the loot. As the pirate smiths drew her hands behind her and riveted slave fetters to her slim yellow wrists, she stood tall almost as a man, looking past her captors with a proud contempt.

"She's a queen!" whispered Cyron. "There was never such a woman!"

He joined the eager pirates that ringed her, staring with an unfeigned admiration. Pillared elaborately upon her proud head, her hair was black and lustrous. Her golden throat and her arms gleamed with jewels of green jade. A torn gown of sheer crimson silk hid few curves of her tall yellow body.

When the one-eyed Tirynthian, who was also the cook, had done hammering the last rivet, he pushed her roughly. She fell, and her bare yellow knees were bruised on the deck. But she uttered no cry of pain, and in spite of the fetters she came back to her feet with a sinuous grace. Her long burning eyes came slowly to one-eyed Vorkos.

"You are now the masters!" She spoke the Cretan tongue, with a limpid singsong accent. "But I am Tai Leng, a princess of far Cathay. I have a talisman of vision, and now I see the angry hand of Minos hanging like a black cloud over you."

Her smoldering eyes swept over the pirate crew, and her proud, yellow shoulders made a little careless shrug. "Before the sun is set," warned her silken tones, "the greatest of you will be a prisoner in the power of Crete."

The one-eyed Tirynthian retreated uneasily, muttering that she was a sorceress and ought therefore to be burned alive. But Cyron hastily objected that no woman so beautiful should be wasted, even so, and the division of the spoil went on.

This partition was made by a method the pirates had devised. White shells were counted out to each man, according to his rank and valor. Then the metal ingots, the slaves, and the other lots of plunder, were auctioned off for shells.

The golden woman went high. Gothung, the blond steersman, organized a group of men to make a collective bid. Cyron offered all his share of shells, a heavy golden belt, and a fine silver bracelet. Finally, adding his precious purple cloak, he bought her.

While the auction was still in progress on the trader, Theseus took the Hittite captain and his men aboard the pirate, and set them safely on the headland as he had promised. Still he was puzzled about the captain. His beady eyes had watched the division of his cargo with apparent unconcern. And they flickered now and then, Theseus had noticed, ever so briefly toward the southwest.

Southwest was the direction of Knossos.

When Theseus went back aboard the prize, he found Cyron standing on the foredeck, staring anxiously in the same direction. The bearded pirate turned with a start.

"Captain Firebrand!" His voice was hoarse. "It is time for us to go. For I have spoken with the yellow girl I bought. And she laughed at me and promised me that tonight will end her captivity. The magic of Minos will rescue her, she says."

His voice dropped apprehensively. "The wizards of Knossos, the yellow girl says, have seen all that has happened. Minos will send a fleet, she says. Through the power of the Dark One, he will make a fair wind to speed the fleet. And he can even make a storm, she told me, to drive us back into the teeth of danger!" Shuddering, Cyron looked fearfully into the southwest.

"It is true," commented Theseus, "that our friend the Hittite captain was watching that quarter very hopefully."

"Then," Cyron demanded, "we shall raise sail while we can?"

"You may, if you think wise," Theseus told him. "But I am going to Knossos."

"To Knossos—in Crete?"

The eyes of Cyron grew big as moons, and he staggered a little backward.

"Not to Knossos! Captain Firebrand, are you mad?"

"Perhaps," said Theseus. "But I am going to Knossos."

"In the name of all the gods," gasped Cyron, "why? The yellow girl told me that Minos has placed a great price upon your head. You are the most feared pirate of the sea. But why walk into a cave of hungry lions?"

Theseus rubbed his lean chin—smooth-shaven with the edge of the Falling Star.

"I talked with the Hittite captain," he said slowly. "What he told me has decided me to go to Knossos. For the nine-year period of the reign of Minos is within two moons of its end, and these slaves and bulls we had taken were intended for the games that take place then."

"But," gasped Cyron, "Captain Firebrand!"

"You must have heard the rule of the Minoan games," said Theseus. "You know that they are played, every nine years, to choose the ruler of Crete. And if any man wins the contests, the old Minos must give up his life, and go down into the dread Labyrinth of the Dark One."

Theseus fingered the hilt of the Falling Star, and a tiny smile touched his lean, bronzed face.

"The winner," he said, "is declared the new Minos. The beauteous Ariadne, the daughter of the old Minos and the vessel of Cybele, will be his to claim. And his will be the Empire of Crete, all the treasure of Knossos, command of the fleets, and even the wizardry of Minos and the Dark One's power."

Cyron stepped back, and his bearded face showed an awed frown. "But I thought, Captain Firebrand," he muttered, "that you sought to destroy the wizardry of Knossos—not to take it for your own!"

Theseus nodded gravely. "I shall destroy them," he said, "when I own them."

Cyron abruptly seized his shoulder and tried to shake him. "Captain Firebrand," he said hoarsely, "are you an utter fool? Don't you know that Minos won the games and his throne a thousand years ago? And that no man has ever had a chance to win, in all the cycles since?"

His voice was dry with dread. "Don't you know that Minos is the greatest of the warlocks? That even the terrible Daedalus serves him? That he is immortal, and destroys with his wizardry all who might hope with skill and daring to win the games?"

"I have heard all that," Theseus said. "But I have never fought in the games at Knossos." His blue eyes smiled. "And the Hittite tells me that Ariadne is very beautiful."

The Dorian answered the grin, grew solemn again. "Captain Firebrand, you can't leave us now." His voice quivered, broke. "It is but a year since you came to our northern rendezvous and begged to join us. But already you are my captain—and my brother."

His dark eyes looked hastily away. "If you must go to Knossos, Captain," he whispered faintly, "then I . . . I'll go with you!"

Theseus smiled again, and took his hand.

"No, Gamecock," he said, "I shall go alone. But cheer up! When the time comes to loot the palace of Minos, perhaps you will be there."

Cyron blinked and grinned. "I'll be there," he choked. Suddenly, then, he started. His dark eyes widened apprehensively again. He stared at Theseus, and then away into the southwest. "Don't joke with me, Captain Firebrand," he begged. "Give the orders, and let us seek the northern islands with our loot."

His pointing arm was trembling. "See the sky in the direction of far Knossos, Captain?" His voice sank hoarsely. "How fair it is? And how angrily the clouds are piling in the north? I have felt the wizardry of Knossos, Captain, and I fear it!"

The blue eyes of Theseus narrowed, swept the horizon. "It is a strange sky!" he said. "But I'm not joking, Captain Gamecock—for you are captain, now. Give your orders, and take your men and the plunder aboard. Let the men divide my share—and you may have the treasure in my cabin. Only leave me the hull of the trader, for I am going to sail to Knossos." He studied the northward sky again. "I think the wind will be favorable enough."

"Captain Firebrand," protested the Dorian, "I wish you wouldn't—"

Theseus turned, stopped the pirate with a sudden pointing gesture. Far away southwestward, across the flat blue sea, stretched a long line of infinitesimal black dots.

"There comes the black-sailed fleet of Minos," Theseus said, "sweeping fast on a changing wind. I am sailing to meet it. And, if you hope to outfly the wizardry of Knossos, Captain Gamecock, you had better take your yellow woman and set sail!"

THREE

THESEUS RETURNED to the pirate for the small leather bag that held his personal effects. Climbing back aboard the prize, he found that the preparations to leave it had halted. A score of the booty-laden pirates were standing in a staring ring about the mast. And Vorkos, the one-eyed Tirynthian cook, was kneeling to fan his fire, heating the point of a long bronze lance.

Theseus pushed through the ring. He found Cyron standing angrily over a small yellow-brown man, who was bound to the mast. The prisoner was squealing in terror, trying to writhe away from another red-hot lance that the enraged pirate was flourishing in front of him.

"Now try your wizardry!" muttered Cyron. "Against hot bronze!"

Theseus stared in astonishment at the captive. He was almost a dwarf. Wide-mouthed, froglike, his wrinkled face was remarkably ugly. Terror had given him a faintly greenish color. His head was completely bald, but he had thick black eyebrows. Huge and yellow and white-rimmed, his eyes were popping out with fear.

"Where did he come from, Captain Gamecock?" asked Theseus.

Cyron sputtered incoherently. Theseus looked wonderingly back at the squealing prisoner. He saw with surprise that the little man was clad in torn fragments of crimson silk, that his scrawny brown arms and neck were laden with green jade and gold.

Theseus caught the angry Dorian's arm.

"The Cretan fleet is coming," he warned. "And the storm is gathering swiftly in the north. If you hope to get away, Gamecock, it is time for you to go!"

Cyron dropped the hot lance on the deck and tried to master his wrath. He glanced apprehensively at the long far line of black sails across the south, and shouted at the cook to hasten his fire.

"We'll be going, Captain Firebrand!" he gasped. "But first I am going to burn the eyes out of this small wizard."

"Where did a wizard come from?" demanded Theseus. "And what happened to your golden woman?"

Cyron gulped for his voice, and kicked viciously at the small brown man's shin.

"There was no golden woman," he muttered. "There was only this evil little wizard. He moaned and picked up his buskined toe, which had struck the mast. "He had taken the woman's guise, to save his cowardly carcass from harm."

He spat at the little brown man.

"I sought to kiss the golden woman, and she changed in my arms. Into—that!" He trembled with rage. "To think that I gave all my share of the prize, and my jewels, and even my purple cloak—to buy a grinning ape!"

He tweaked the small man's nose.

"Anyhow, I shall have the pleasure of burning out his eyes —and I am going to enjoy it!"

The prisoner emitted another screech, and twisted desperately against the ropes. His bulging, yellow eyes rolled fearfully, and fastened upon Theseus.

"O, Captain Firebrand!" His voice was a high nasal whine. "O greatest of the pirates, whose honor and audacity are spoken even in my own far Babylon! Oh, save me!"

Theseus hooked thumbs in his belt, and shook his red head. "I don't like wizards."

The yellow eyes blinked at him hopefully. "But I am the most insignificant and powerless of wizards," came the frantic piping plea. "My spells are only the feeblest and most useless. None of them can harm any man. If I possessed the powers of the warlocks of Knossos, would I be here, bound, tortured?"

The yellow eyes rolled fearfully to Cyron, and Theseus stepped a little nearer. "So you were the golden princess?"

"I was," whined the little man. "That spell is the greatest of my powers, and even it is feeble. For every touch weakens it, and a kiss will break it." He was watching Cyron, and his voice became a frantic gasping. "I meant no harm, Captain Firebrand. I used the guise only to save my miserable life. Aid me, Captain, and I shall be your slave. You can command my tiny magic. Only save—"

Cyron came back with a red-hot lance, and his voice lifted into a shriek.

Theseus gestured the angry pirate back. "Wait, Captain Gamecock," he begged. "Let me speak to this small wizard. There is a saying that magic is best fought with magic. And I fight the wizardry of Crete."

Cyron flourished the glowing blade impatiently. "But I bought this wizard," he muttered. "Surely his eyes are mine, to burn out when I like. And probably his spells will be just as useful after he is blind."

The little man squalled thinly.

"All the treasure in my cabin is yours, Gamecock," said Theseus. "You can buy one of the blond slaves."

"They are not the golden princess," muttered Cyron. "But you may speak to him, before I enjoy the small pleasure that his wizard's trick has left me."

Theseus stepped closer to the squirming prisoner, asking: "Who are you, and how came you aboard?"

"My name is Snish," whined the little yellow-brown man, eagerly. "I was born in far-off Babylon. There are many wizards and sorcerers in Babylon. But none of them is so great as the least warlock of Crete. And I was the smallest and feeblest of them all."

"In that case," inquired Theseus, "why were you sailing to Crete?"

"It is an unfortunate matter of the weather," Snish told him.

"The weather?"

The little wizard rolled anxious yellow eyes at Cyron. "Only the most advanced and gifted sorcerers can actually rule the elements," he explained uneasily. "Minor magicians, however, have sometimes been able to establish substantial reputations upon the natural uncertainties of the weather, merely through fortunate coincidence.

"Now it was one very dry summer when I embarked upon my career in Babylon. The fields were parched about the city, the canals were dry, and the river was too low for irrigation. Under such circumstances, I was unwise enough to undertake contracts to bring rain.

"Every similar drought, I knew, had been ended at last by rain—and some enterprising magician had been able to claim the credit for it. Therefore, I built a mud tower in the fields, and burned herbs on the top of it, and sacrificed a kid, and kept vigils under the stars, and waited, like the farmers, for rain to come.

"But there was never such a drought in Babylon. The sky by day was like a hot copper bowl, and the stars were jewels at night. The young corn withered and blew away on the wind, and the starved cattle died, and men with donkeys made fortunes selling muddy water in the streets of Babylon.

"My clients began to grow impatient. In vain I discussed with them the phenomenal difficulties that faced my enterprise, and trebled my fees. Finally they demanded the return of all they had paid me. The money, unfortunately, was already spent. But my clients departed, without it, and took their problem to another magician.

"This other magician was a stranger, who had arrived in Babylon only recently—almost on the day, in fact, that the drought began. Very little was known of him. But a sudden rumor had swept the city that he came from Crete, and had studied the arts of Daedalus and Minos.

"The stranger offered, for a fabulous sum, to bring rain on this very night. My former clients were desperate. They went to the Hittite usurers, pledged their lands and slaves and cattle and even their wives, and borrowed the stranger's fee.

"That night it rained.

"I knew then that the stranger possessed the power that I had claimed, and that his superior arts must in fact have been responsible for my failure. I sought for him, intending to ask him to take me for an apprentice. But I found that he had already departed. None knew how or where he had gone, but a huge strange bird had been seen rising through the storm clouds.

"Returning through the muddy streets to my own dwelling, I found that some of my angry clients had come there to insist upon return of their fees. I found it therefore expedient to assume the guise of a woman and leave Babylon also, astride a donkey."

The Dorian pirate made an impatient gesture with his smoking lance. The little wizard shuddered in the ropes that bound him to the mast, and Theseus held out a restraining hand.

"Wait till you know my peculiar misfortune," begged Snish. "The stranger from Knossos must have cast some powerful spell upon me, which he neglected to lift before he departed. For all matters concerning the weather remain unfortunate for me.

"My travels since I left Babylon have been extensive and

usually unwilling. I was put ashore near Troy some moons ago by an Egyptian captain who had begun to suspect that my presence aboard his ship had something to do with unfavorable winds."

Cyron came with a hot lance from the fire. "Let me at him, Captain Firebrand," he begged. "The Cretan fleet is bearing down upon us—this lying little wizard is trying to talk us all to death. Let me burn his eyes out, and go."

"Wait, Gamecock." Theseus stopped him, and turned back to the shuddering little wizard. "If you have such cause to fear the warlocks of Knossos," he said, "you had better explain why you were sailing for Crete! And talk fast!"

Snish rolled his bulging yellow eyes. "I was coming to that," he wheezed anxiously. "I found myself friendless in Troy. In Babylon, before I so unwisely sought to change my trade, I had been a cobbler. I sought employment in the shops of Troy, but I could find nothing, and hunger presently forced me to make a living with my small arts. I began to make certain prophecies to the clients who came to me—with results that proved unfortunate."

Snish shook his bald, brown head regretfully, and his eyes rolled at Cyron, who was watching the southward sea and flourishing the hot lance with increasing impatience.

"You see, even Troy has been compelled to yield tribute to Minos, and many were inquisitive about the future of Crete. Now, whatever one may actually read of the future—and it is said that the warlocks of Crete can survey it with considerable certainty—it is almost invariably the best policy for the seer to ignore his actual findings, and tell his clients merely what they wish to believe.

"I assured the Trojans, therefore, that Minos is doomed, and that all the splendor of Crete will one day be forgotten, and that Troy will one day be the mistress of the world—I ignored certain grave indications in the stars as to the fate of Troy itself, save to warn the Trojans to beware of horses.

"I had no rivals in Troy, for it is but a small city, and for a time I was very successful. Too successful, in fact, for my fame reached the ears of the Cretan resident. He sent for a Cretan priest, and the priest had me arrested."

Snish shuddered against the ropes. "It appears," he said, "that all the practitioners of magic in the dominions of Minos are organized in a compact and jealous guild. No wizard outside the guild is allowed to practice. Unwittingly, I broke the law. I was being taken to Knossos, to face what is called the justice of the Dark One."

The little Babylonian trembled and turned slightly green. "Perhaps you have heard ot the justice of the Dark One," he gasped. "It is the most fearful fate that can befall a human being. For the victim is sent beyond human justice. He is thrust into the black Labyrinth, beneath the palace of Minos, that is the dwelling of the Dark One. And that evil deity, it is said, devours both body and soul of all who enter there."

Snish repressed another shudder, and blinked hopefully at Theseus. "I had induced the Hittite captain to post a bond for me," his shrill voice hurried on. "And I hoped that he could be persuaded to escape from the convoy tonight, and sail for Egypt. But that would have brought all the wizardry of Knossos upon my trail."

The yellow eyes of Snish followed Cyron's smoking lances. "It is most fortunate for me, Captain Firebrand, that you took the ship," he wheezed hastily. "That is, if you can dissuade this pirate from his evil intent toward the smallest, the kindest, and the most insignificant of wizards. Save me, Captain Firebrand!" His voice became a squeal. "Let my small magic serve you!"

Cyron tugged at the arm of Theseus, and his fingers trembled. "Let me at the wizard," he begged huskily. "For the fleet is coming fast, and the northward sky has an evil look."

"Wait, Gamecock," urged Theseus. "Perhaps I can use his magic."

Snish stirred hopefully in the ropes. "Indeed you can, Captain Firebrand." His yellow eyes lifted to the rising black clouds. "And I suggest, Captain Gamecock," he shrilled, "that you had better leave me, soon. Because, as I told you, I have difficulty with the weather. That storm is doubtless following me."

Apprehension had mounted above Cyron's cooling wrath. He flung his smoking pike down upon the deck, and shouted at his men to make ready with the sail. "Take him, Captain Firebrand," he muttered. "But watch him. For no wizard can be trusted—not even such a cowardly dog of a wizard as this!"

He leaped to the pirate's deck, and axes flashed to cut the lashings. "Farewell, Captain Firebrand!" His shout came hoarse and strained. "Beware the wizard!"

The red sail went up—for there was still a breath of wind in the south. The Mycenean's long whip came to hissing life, and flashing oars pulled the galley toward the northward strait, to meet the coming storm.

Alone with Snish on the prize, for even the oar slaves had been herded aboard the pirate, Theseus cut the ropes that had bound the little wizard, and sent him to take the steering oars.

Theseus himself climbed the stays and loosed the huge yellow sail to the fitful wind. He had it spread by the time the south wind died and the first cold blast of the storm struck from the north.

"Which way, Captain Firebrand?" came the anxious piping of Snish. "Shall we steer to the east, and seek to escape the Cretans under the darkness of the storm?"

The head of Theseus lifted high, and his red hair whipped in the wind. He looked across the sea, at a long line of black sails advancing upon that amazing south wind. At last he turned, grave-eyed, back to the little wizard.

"No," he said quietly. "Steer straight to meet them."

The brown frog-face turned faintly green once more, and then gnarled hands trembled on the steering oar. "Aye, Captain Firebrand," wheezed Snish, "we steer straight to meet them." His bald head shook ominously. "But my feeble arts tell me that I should have done better to remain with the Gamecock, even at the cost of my eyes!"

FOUR

LOOKING AFT again, when he had the square yellow sail securely set, Theseus was not greatly surprised to see that Snish, at the steering oars, had resumed his feminine guise.

Tai Leng smiled at him, with a smoldering light in her long, almond eyes. A provocative twist of her tall, golden body moved Theseus briefly to inquire whether the spell might not be made proof against destruction by contact.

The yellow princess shook her head. "The guise is merely a measure of safety," commented her soft singsong. "Even a woman is exposed to certain dangers. But a sufficient beauty can usually evade them."

Approaching her, Theseus fancied that he saw in her yellow features some faint mocking hint of the frog-face of Snish. And the limpid singsong, when she spoke again, had a slight nasal undertone.

"Shall I not disguise you, also, Captain Firebrand?" she asked. "My insignificant arts are at your command."

Theseus shook his head. "I seek to destroy the arts of wizardry, not to employ them." He shrugged wearily. "Anyhow, the overthrow of the throne of Minos is no task for women."

"The guise need not be a woman's," the yellow girl assured him. "That is merely the one which best insures my own safety. I can give you the likeness of any man you choose."

Theseus stared at the black sails marching from the south, before that mysterious wind. "There is the black priest I killed." He rubbed reflectively at his lean chin. "No," he said abruptly. "In time, such a guise might be useful. But now I am going to meet the Cretans as the pirate, Captain Firebrand, with the Falling Star to speak for me."

The long, almond eyes of Tai Leng smoldered, inscrutable. "But Captain Firebrand is already wanted," her silken voice protested. "Minos has offered ten talents of silver for your head—"

The singsong ceased abruptly; something glittered in her smoky eyes.

"Seek to collect it," warned Theseus, grimly, "and no wizard's guise will save your guts from being spilled by the Falling Star!"

To emphasize the warning, he seized the soft yellow curve of a shoulder exposed by the torn crimson silk and shook vigorously. The result was a strange transformation.

The yielding golden flesh changed under his fingers; became brown, bony. The exotic woman's face melted halfway into the ugly frog-features of Snish, and the protesting voice had a nasal whine: "Captain Firebrand, can't you trust me? For I owe you my eyes, and even my life. I am your smallest, most miserable, most devoted slave."

"I trust no wizard—not even if he is small enough to be a louse on my belly," muttered Theseus. "However, your arts may be useful to me—puny as they are against the wizardry of Knossos. I shall not destroy you—yet."

The golden princess dropped on her knees and kissed his hand. He felt her lips change, as they pressed against his fingers. And for a moment the black lustrous pile of her perfumed hair was gone, and he saw the brown bald head of Snish.

"Go back to your steering oar," Theseus told her. "The word of a wizard is nothing; but, so long as we are both enemies of Knossos, perhaps we can serve one another."

He threw hay to the three great black bulls, bellowing in their narrow pen. Eying the graceful danger of their tapered tossing horns, he thought of the games to be played for the throne of Minos, and could not help a little shudder. For many perils lay before the throne, and those horns were but the symbol of the Dark One's monstrous power.

Driven before the storm, the trader plowed on southward. The fleet came before that strange south wind to meet her, and narrow black hulls lifted beneath the black square sails.

Black bull's-head standards came into view, and at last Theseus could see the purple streamer that marked the flagship. He commanded the yellow woman to steer toward it. Tai Leng silently obeyed. Her yellow face was pale, and fear distended her long, oblique eyes.

The cold storm wind faltered and died as the fleet drew near. The galley wallowed, yellow sail slack, in a sudden calm. The south wind that brought the Cretans had ceased also, and glinting oars brought the flagship across the last arrow's flight.

"Ahoy!" shouted a brass-lunged officer. "What ship spreads the yellow sail of Amur the Hittite?"

Theseus cupped bronze hands to his face. "This ship is a prize of war," he returned. "Her captain is the free Achean, Captain Firebrand. He sails to Crete, with a gift of three black bulls for the Minoan games, and a yellow princess of Cathay to grace the megaron of Minos. But what ship spreads the black sail of Knossos?"

There was a startled pause before: "This ship," the officer bellowed, "is the flagship of the north fleet of Minos, who is himself a god and companion of the Dark One, who is also ruler of Crete and the isles of the sea and the coasts beyond. And her commander is Phaistro, first noble of Knossos and admiral of all the fleets of Minos."

The ships touched. A squad of Cretan marines, armed with nets and tridents, leaped to the trader's deck and made a watchful circle about Theseus. When the ships were lashed, Phaistro himself followed.

The admiral was tall for a Cretan, but small-boned and wiry. His swarthy face was thinly aristocratic, almost handsome. Theseus looked at the feeble chin, the full red lips and the dark, sullen eyes. He saw the lines in the face, the nervous tension of the body. For all his passion and his pride, Theseus thought, this man was yet a weakling.

With a walk that had a certain womanish grace, Phaistro crossed the deck. Theseus caught the perfume of his dark hair, which was dressed in the elaborate Cretan fashion, with three coils on the head and three long curls behind.

The admiral's attire was rich and almost femininely dainty. His loose ceremonial robe was the purple of his rank. Parted in the front, it showed his tight-drawn golden belt and white linen loincloth. He wore tall, embroidered buskins, and his bare, brown arms were laden with gold and silver bracelets.

Surrounded with a little group of officers, who held ready hands on their swords, the admiral paused before Theseus. His narrow face seemed to reflect a certain unwilling admiration. "So you are the famous Captain Firebrand?"

"Men call me that," said Theseus.

"Then where is your swift galley, that has taken so many prizes?" Suddenly piercing, the dark eyes of the admiral studied Theseus. "And where are your reckless men?"

"Ask your wizards," Theseus said.

Phaistro caught his breath, and anger glittered in his eyes. "Where is this ship's crew?" His voice crackled. "And all the treasure from the north coasts that was aboard? And where are the two royal convoys?"

Theseus grinned. "The Hittite and his men are safe on the headland behind us," he said. "As for the treasure and the convoys, ask your wizards again. Or go fishing on the bottom of the sea!"

The admiral made a sputtering sound, and trembled in the purple robe. "Captain Firebrand"—his voice came tense and sharp—"we have heard of you at Knossos—"

"—And you'll hear more," Theseus promised quietly. "Because I am sailing for Crete, with gifts for Minos." He nodded at the wild black bulls in their pen on the deck, at the

31

tall yellow girl by the steering oar. "And I am going to enter the cyclic games," he said, "as a candidate for the throne of Minos."

The admiral stiffened. For a moment he was breathless, his dark eyes wide with astonishment. Then he bent convulsively, and his thin face turned red, and he cackled with shrill laughter. He turned to the Cretan officers about him, small dark men with broad leather belts and black loincloths, gasping through his laughter: "The pirate says he is going to enter the games, to seek the throne of Minos. Isn't that a capital joke?"

Evidently it was. The officers doubled themselves with merriment—without neglecting, however, to keep watchful eyes on Theseus and ready hands near their swords. At last the admiral sobered his thin face and turned back to Theseus.

"I'm sure, Captain Firebrand," he said, weak-voiced from laughter, "that your battles with bulls and men and the gods will make a very interesting spectacle. But don't you think you are somewhat rash to volunteer, when no man has won the games in the last hundred cycles?"

"It seems to me," Theseus said, "that Minos is the rash one, to keep repeating the games. But what is your joke?"

Phaistro laughed again, until tears came into his eyes. "The joke . . . the joke is very simple," he panted at last. "You tell us that you are sailing to Crete to enter the Minoan games. And the orders of the fleet, Captain Firebrand, were to bring you to Knossos—to be flung into the games!"

"If that is a joke," said Theseus, "aren't you perhaps laughing ahead of the point?"

Phaistro flushed red again with anger. His thin hands clenched and his dark eyes glittered. After a moment, however, he gulped and tried to smile at the tall Achean.

"I forgive your insolence, Captain Firebrand, because you are a brave man," he said. "And I am going to offer you a piece of advice—again because your audacity moves me."

Phaistro stepped quickly forward from his officers, and: "Don't surrender your sword," he urged quickly, in a lowered voice. "Don't let us take you alive to Knossos! Better throw yourself upon your own blade, and die cleanly outside the shadow of the Dark One."

Theseus touched his sword, smiling. "Thank you, admiral," he said softly. "And I shall not surrender the Falling Star. But neither shall I kill myself." He drew the long steel blade out of its scabbard. "I am going to carry the Falling Star to Crete."

Phaistro's thin face turned dark again. "Pirate, your impudence has gone too far," he snapped angrily. "Give up your sword—or my men will take it."

Theseus lifted the blade. "Let them try!" His blue eyes smiled warily. "There are wizards outside Knossos," he said softly. "One of them, admiral, is my slave. And my sword was forged from a burning star. It is an enchanted blade, and it will cut any other. If you want it—take it!"

Phaistro's dark eyes flickered uncertainly aside at the tall golden form of Tai Leng, standing lazily beside the steering oar. They roved the empty decks, and came uneasily back to Theseus and the brandished Falling Star.

Theseus watched the admiral's narrow face. It still had the tensity of anger, but the pallor of fear was now upon it, too. Phaistro was obviously afraid of wizardry. And it must seem strange, Theseus knew, to meet a ship sailed by two alone: such a man as he was, and such a woman as Tai Leng.

The full red lips of the admiral quivered uncertainly. His thin hands clenched and opened, and tugged uncertainly at the edges of his purple robe. And his awe of magic at last prevailed.

"If your weapon is indeed protected by enchantment," he yielded at last, "then you can carry it until we touch Crete. There Minos and his wizards can break the spell soon enough. And no doubt brazen Talos can take it from you, if he must. For no man carries any weapon into the Minoan games."

"We shall see," Theseus said, "when we come to Crete."

Phaistro made a gesture toward the flagship. "Now, Captain Firebrand," he said, "come aboard my vessel. You will be my guest of honor, until we land. I'll leave a crew to sail this ship. The priests will be waiting for you at the docks."

Theseus shook his head. "This ship is my prize," he said quietly. "I am sailing her to Crete, carrying gifts to Minos, and I require no aid. I'll deal with Minos and his priests when I meet them."

Dark red of anger mounted once more into the admiral's thin face. His quivering mouth opened for some command. But his eyes dwelt anxiously upon the bright ready sword of

Theseus and the strange yellow beauty of Tai Leng. Abruptly he muttered something to his officers, led them back toward the flagship.

"Sail on, Captain Firebrand!" Phaistro shouted hoarsely from his own deck. "We shall follow you to Knossos."

His marines cast the lashings loose. Theseus and the golden woman were left once more alone upon the prize.

"Beware, Captain Firebrand!" The melodious singsong of Tai Leng carried a faint whining undertone of Snish. "Those who claim enchantments which they don't possess are indeed in danger from the warlocks of Knossos. I know!"

"We shall see," Theseus repeated, "when we arrive in Crete."

The south wind that brought the fleet had dropped into an utter calm. But the black mountain of the storm still loomed in the north, and now a fresh cold wind blew out of it again. The yellow sail filled. And the Cretan ships came about and sailed close to the prize, back toward Knossos.

That change of the wind, Theseus knew, was a perfectly natural thing. A thousand times he had seen the wind blow against a storm, and die, and rise again out of the cloud. And yet he could not help a shudder, at the way the winds seemed to serve the wizardry of Crete.

The sun had not yet set when another long galley came out of the southwest. It bore no sail, and the mast was unshipped, for it came against the wind. But swift-flashing oars brought it on at racing speed, and presently Theseus could see that its standard was the golden eagle of Amur the Hittite.

The galley hailed the black flagship. The admiral's sail was briefly lowered, and oars brought the two vessels prow to prow. Two men leaped across to the flagship, and the black sail went up again.

Across two arrow-flights of water, Theseus watched the two strangers hurry aft. He could see that one of them wore the long black robe of a Minoan priest, that the other was garbed in the yellow of Amur.

The admiral, in his own purple, met them before his high cabin. The priest handed him something thin and white. He unrolled it, into a papyrus scroll. For a few moments he was motionless, as if reading. Then the three began waving their hands excitedly.

No word of their conversation reached Theseus. But he

34

saw each of them, in turn, point in his direction. He was wondering, with growing apprehension, what they were talking about, when the liquid voice of Tai Leng softly called: "Captain Firebrand!"

Theseus turned to the tall yellow woman leaning on the steering oar. Her smooth exotic face was intent, her long slanted eyes fixed on the distant group. Again Theseus found space to regret that her allure was all illusion.

"Captain, you wish to know what they say of you?"

"Of course I do." Theseus stepped quickly to her side—and saw that mocking hint of Snish come back into her golden beauty. "You can tell?"

"Eavesdropping is among the simplest bits of magic," Tai Leng assured him—and her singsong had a nasal hint of Snish. "Even I have mastered that. Except, of course, that I cannot eavesdrop upon a more powerful magician."

"Well," demanded Theseus, "what are they saying?"

"The priest has brought a letter from Minos to the admiral. He read it aloud. It contains new orders with regard to your fate, Captain Firebrand."

Theseus glanced apprehensively back at the three. "And what are the new orders?"

"Evidently Minos has consulted the screed of the future—and discovered that he was unwise in ordering you to be brought to Knossos for the games. Because the letter contains orders that you are to be slain at once."

The hand of Theseus slipped automatically toward the Falling Star. "Your body," Tai Leng went on, "is to be sealed in a lead-lined casket, and secured by certain powerful talismans that the priest has brought with him, and dropped into the sea where it is deep.

"Only your sword is to be carried back to Knossos, as proof that you are dead." The golden princess shuddered. "That makes matters appear very grave," said her nasal singsong. "For both of us."

FIVE

"AND WHAT," inquired Theseus, "are they saying now?"

The slanted smoldering eyes of the golden girl—which showed, when Theseus looked closely, a curious yellow hint of the popping eyes of Snish—peered back at the three long-robed men on the other galley.

"The yellow-robe," Tai Leng told him, "is Amur the Hittite, himself. He is the richest man in the world, and probably the most crafty. He is no wizard, but his wealth can bind warlocks to serve him."

"I've heard of Amur," said Theseus. "What does he want?"

"Amur," said the yellow woman, "learned of the same prescience that caused Minos to dispatch the new orders for your death. And the Hittite, being a crafty man, formed a scheme to turn the situation into silver and gold."

"And what is the scheme?"

Tai Leng watched for a while, silently. "Amur is unwilling to reveal his plan, before the Minoan priest," she said at last. "But soon you will know. Because he and the admiral are coming aboard, to speak with you."

Theseus saw that the flagship was veering toward them.

"Whatever his plot is," warned her nasal singsong, "it means no more good for you than the papyrus from Minos. For Amur is sometimes called the scorpion, and his craft is a venom that poisons men."

Once again the Cretan marines grappled the trader, lashed it to the flagship. Small brown officers assisted Admiral Phaistro and Amur the Hittite over the rails. Theseus walked to meet them, staring curiously at the Hittite.

Amur was a swarthy man, with the powerful hooked nose of his race. His dark eyes were beady, cunning, set too close together. Shaven, in the Cretan fashion, his face had a blood-less, waxen look. His limbs were thin, but his body seemed fat, bloated. He was laden with golden jewelry. His hungry eyes flashed about the empty decks, then glittered at Theseus with a concentrated malice.

"This is my ship, that my nephew commanded!" His voice had a husky, whispering quality. "Where is the amber and tin and silver that he brought from the north coasts? And the bales of fur, and the blond slaves?"

"You might go fishing for them," Theseus grinned. "Or ask the wizards."

Amur stepped close to Theseus, and his eyes glittered craftily. "I have asked the wizards," his dry voice rasped. "I climbed to the high tower of the great Daedalus himself, and paid him five talents of silver for the spinning of his shining ball—the warlocks think of nothing but robbing honest men with their fees!

"But he showed me your red-sailed galley, Captain Firebrand, fleeing up into the islands with my treasure. I have spoken to Phaistro, who is my friend." Amur leered at the purple-robed admiral. "And another fleet will be dispatched, upon a favorable wind, to intercept the pirate."

His hands drew into thin, tense claws, and Theseus saw that the yellow fingers were heavy with golden rings.

"All my treasure will be recovered," grated the flat voice of Amur. "To the last grain of silver! The pirates will be captured, for my slave pens." The small eyes gleamed. "And you, Captain Firebrand, shall restore my five talents of silver—twenty times over."

Theseus waited, thoughtfully fingering the inlaid hilt of the Falling Star. Here was another type of man, it came to him, whose power was almost as evil as wizardry. Amur stepped back from him, anxiously.

"Hold your blade, Captain Firebrand," he rasped anxiously. "For I have come to save your life." He came nearer, dropped his voice. "The warlocks have read the tablets of time," he whispered swiftly. "They find indications of your victory if you enter the Minoan games."

Theseus touched the Falling Star, and grinned. "I read the same omens in my blade," he said.

The close-set eyes of Amur narrowed. "Minos has dispatched orders for your death," he rasped. "But I have come to save your life for the games. For Minos requires no proof of your death but your sword, and the body of a slave can fill the weighted box we sink into the sea."

Theseus grinned again. "Your own body could!"

Amur flinched, but his hoarse whisper raced on: "I shall

37

take you to Crete aboard my own galley. And there is a wizard in Ekoros who has certain things to hide. For a few talents of silver—and to save his cowardly life—he will turn you into a black Nubian. I shall send the Nubian to Minos from my slave pens, a gift for the games. And the Nubian—unless the warlocks have lied—will win."

"But how," demanded Theseus, "do you make any money out of that?"

The small black eyes of Amur shone hungrily. "The Minoan games are divided into nine contests," his swift whisper rasped. "One for each year of the cycle. You must face three wild bulls, three fighting men, and three gods. And it is a custom of the nobles and the merchants of Crete to place wagers on each contest."

Amur laced gold-ringed fingers across his belly. "How an unarmed man can win those nine contests, I don't know. That is your problem. But Minos must believe you can. And my black Nubian will win all that is wagered that day!"

Theseus turned slowly from Amur to Phaistro. The purple-robed admiral had been looking on, silently. His thin face seemed pale, tortured.

"What do you say of this, admiral?" demanded Theseus. "Minos has ordered you to kill me."

Amur laid a cold hand on the arm of Theseus, and rasped an answer for the admiral: "He will do as I request, Captain Firebrand. I am no warlock, yet even I possess a certain power. The noble Phaistro will do whatever I ask, even if I require him to cut off his hand. Is that not true, admiral?"

The red lips of Phaistro trembled, and he nodded unhappily.

The cold, bright snake-eyes of Amur came back to Theseus. "You see, Captain Firebrand, my scheme has neglected nothing. Now give up your sword to the admiral, and come aboard my galley—and soon you will be mounting the gilded throne of Minos!"

Theseus reached for the hilt of the Falling Star. He drew the long blade from its sheath, and looked down into the gleaming mirror of its polish, and saw there the sad face of his father.

It was on that solemn night, many years ago, when proud Athens had bowed at last to the ships and the wizardry of Knossos. His father, the Achean king, was wearily pacing his long stone-flagged hall in the simple palace upon the Acropolis. Faintly they could hear the women, in their quarters, wailing for the men who had died that day.

Theseus followed the tired limping steps of Aegeus. "I know you had to yield, father," he said. "I saw the blue shining bolts that struck down your captains. I know your men fled from the sorcery of Crete. The truce saved Athens from being burned, saved your people from being carried off to feed the evil god of Knossos.

"But I am not going to give up, father!"

The wounded king paused and looked down at him. "But you . . . you are only a slip of a lad, Theseus—you can't well defy an empire whose ruler is a god."

"Yes, I can, father. I am going away tonight, toward the far lands that are still free from Crete. I shall train myself to be brave and strong, and grow up to be a fighting man. And I shall make war on Minos, so long as I live!"

A smile came to the king's haggard face. "I am glad, my son," Aegeus said softly. "You have made me happy again. And I shall give you my sword to carry with you—if you are strong enough to lift the stone where it is hidden from the Cretans."

The king limped to point out the heavy flagstone. Theseus eagerly caught the edges of it, and pried and strained until at last it turned over. His father took up the sword, and gave it to him, and he admired the bright color of its steel.

"It is named the Falling Star," the king told him, "because its strange bright metal fell from the sky. The lame smith who forged it was a very wise man, and he hammered a simple spell into the blade.

"It will guard the freedom of the Greeks, the smith promised me; hew their way to greatness. But it must never be surrendered. For the man who gives it up, yields also his honor and his life."

Trembling with pride, Theseus swung the blade. It was heavy for his young arm, and the hilt too large for his hand. But he rejoiced in the cold weight of it, and the magical fire that ran along its edge.

"I thank you, father," he whispered. "I shall never give up the Falling Star. And I shall carry it against the wizardry of Knossos, and fight for the freedom of the Greeks, so long as I can lift it!"

He wept as he embraced his father, and took the heavy

sword, and went out into the night. He slipped past the watch fire of the Cretan sentries, climbed by a way he knew down the steep slope of the Acropolis, and ran away through the darkness that lay upon the conquered plain of Attica.

Now, in the mirror of the blade, Theseus could see the yellow robe of Amur and the admiral's purple. They moved impatiently.

"Give up the sword," rapped the sharp tones of Phaistro, "or I shall signal my archers to draw—and bury you at sea as Minos commanded."

"Choose!" rasped the Hittite. "Life and victory and the throne of Minos—or death!" His eyes flickered uneasily into the north. "And quickly. For the warlocks are sending a storm to hasten us home."

Theseus saw an angry blade of lightning stab from the dark wall of cloud to northward. His eyes came back to Tai Leng, found the yellow woman standing by the steering oar, stiff and pale as if with dread. His lean body drew straight with decision.

"If you want the Falling Star"—he grinned at Amur and the admiral—"you'll have to take it!"

The hawk-nosed face of Amur drew into a yellow mask of evil wrath. Dark with anger, the admiral turned, as if to signal his waiting archers. But Theseus, with a gesture at the storm cloud, stopped him.

"Wait a moment, admiral—if you hope to see dry land again!"

The two watched mistrustfully as Theseus beckoned to Tai Leng. Moving with a lazy queenly grace, the yellow woman left the steering oar, and came to him. A gust of cold wind fluttered the torn crimson silk against her tall body.

"Snish," commanded Theseus, "resume your true form!"

Her golden face went pale with fear.

"But—my master—"

"Obey," ordered Theseus. "Or I shall touch you."

"Master," sobbed Tai Leng, "my life and my art are yours!"

Abruptly, then, squat little Snish was standing where she had stood, with the tattered silk whipping about his gnarled brown figure.

Six

THE SEAMED frog-face of Snish was as pale, almost, as the yellow girl's had been, and his huge yellow eyes were bulging with dread. Faintly, his thin voice whined:

"Captain Firebrand, what do you require of your most insignificant slave?"

Standing beside him, Theseus whispered: "I think that your difficulty with the weather is going to save both our lives!"

He turned to Amur and the admiral. Both of them had already betrayed awe of the warlock's art. Now Phaistro's thin face was pale and rigid. Amur, waxen-cheeked, was desperately breathing some incantation.

"I'm afraid that you have misled yourselves," Theseus told them. "For the storm approaching us is not the work of Minos at all—nor of anyone, admiral, who will be very tender with your ships."

He gestured at the angry avalanche of black cloud rolling down from the north, and then at the shuddering Snish.

"This is my own wizard," he announced, and lifted his voice above a rumble of thunder. "He is a most remarkable Babylonian sorcerer, and he is responsible for this storm. Tell them, Snish!"

The little wizard nodded his brown bald head, apprehensively. He made a fearful little obeisance toward Amur and the admiral. "Masters, that is true," he croaked against the roar of a rising wind. "The storm follows me!"

Casting an uneasy eye at the storm, the admiral stiffened angrily.

"Nonsense!" he rapped sharply. "You can see the dwarf is scared to death. I'll yield to no such trick. Your sword, Captain Firebrand, or your life!"

But Amur was tugging fearfully at his arm. "All wizards are cowards," rasped the Hittite. "Beware!"

"Beware!" echoed Theseus, and whitecaps flashed ominously across the northward sea. Great sudden drops of rain spattered the deck, and the wind struck savagely. Strained rigging creaked and the galley heeled far over.

"Cut us free," Theseus shouted, against the bellow of wind and thunder, "while you can!"

Amur and the admiral scrambled up the sloping deck, tumbled back aboard the flagship. Marines with axes hewed desperately at the lashings. The vessels parted, and the sea flung them back together with an ominous crash.

Running to aid Snish with the steering oar, Theseus crouched beneath a flight of arrows. But most of the Cretans were already busy reefing sail.

Theseus leaned on a steering oar, and the racing galley heeled until the waves washed her gunwales. Her lifted hull caught the second flight of arrows. Then the flagship's black sail split with a boom, and she was left behind.

"Captain Firebrand!" gasped Snish, who had not resumed his feminine guise, "cut loose the sail! Or we'll capsize!"

Theseus flung his strength against the oar, and the vessel rode up out of a yawning trough. Snish turned green and doubled over the rail. The wind whipped torn red silk about his shuddering brown body.

In the dusky, unreal light of the storm, they drew ahead of the fleet. A lightning flash revealed the black hulls, scattered and tossing, sails chewed up and oarsmen fighting the storm. And then they were hidden beyond a curtain of rain.

Night fell above the cloud, and blue twilight thickened to inky blackness. The battered galley groaned, and dipped until water buried her foredeck. But Theseus stood by Snish at the steering oars, and took her through the storm until its first violence began to slacken.

"We shall reach the coast of Crete," Theseus shouted, "before this wind has died."

Snish came stumbling weakly back from the rail. "So we may, Captain Firebrand," he croaked weakly. "We may be flung upon it in the darkness, and broken on the rocks." A last flicker of lightning showed his huge-mouthed face, eloquent with apprehension. "Let us bear to the east," he gasped hoarsely. "This wind will carry us around the end of Crete by dawn. And beyond lies Egypt."

"But Crete is our destination."

Snish was sick again. "Egypt is a better one," he wheezed from the rail. "It is an ancient land, Captain Firebrand, and wealthy. Its gods dwell elsewhere and seldom trouble men, and their priests have no such evil powers as the warlocks of Knossos."

He stumbled back to Theseus. "With your sword, Captain Firebrand, and my small arts," he croaked hopefully, "we can win wealth and renown for ourselves in Egypt. We can earn lands and slaves and honor."

"That may be," agreed Theseus. "But we are going to Crete. You heard the scroll. You know that Minos himself has foreseen that I shall win the games. And send him into the Labyrinth to seek the mercy of his own dark god! And claim for myself his gilded throne and the charms of fair Ariadne—to enjoy until I can overwhelm the Dark One and end the reign of wizardry!"

The quivering hand of Snish caught his arm in the darkness. "But Minos is strong on his throne," protested the little wizard, "and he has held it for a thousand years. While times are unsettled in Egypt, and the Pharaoh himself trembles before the press of invaders from the north. Why not join with those invaders, Captain Firebrand? You might even become the new Pharaoh."

"We are going to Knossos."

"But consider the folly of that," Snish croaked urgently. "It is not quickness nor courage, nor even battle craft, that wins in the Minoan games. It is magic. And Minos is the oldest and greatest magician. He is himself a god! Therefore he always wins—and they who seek his throne always perish before his wizardry."

Theseus peered into the gloom that lay upon the tossing sea. "We shall see," he said. "Already we have passed the fleet."

"But the fleet is merely the wooden wall of unwalled Knossos," argued Snish. "There is Talos, the giant of brass, that the Cretans call the second wall. And Talos alone could break down the walls of any city, or scatter any army that ever marched.

"Even if you should pass by Talos, there is the secret that is called the wall of wizardry. It is known only to Minos and his daughter Ariadne. But its strange power is stronger than the fleet, and stronger than the giant of brass."

Cold and trembling, the hand of Snish tightened on Theseus' arm. "Now, Captain Firebrand," he croaked hopefully, "shall we sail for Egypt?"

"We shall, small wizard." Theseus laughed. "After we have

destroyed Minos, and broken the power of the Dark One."

"Then"—and the teeth of Snish were chattering—"we shall never see Egypt!"

The night wore on, and the north wind continued to blow. Theseus sent Snish to the cabin to sleep, and steered the ship alone. At last, far to westward, he saw a light that burned strangely red and green.

The light was a beacon fire, he knew, kindled on a tower on the headland, to guide the ships of Crete to the harbor below Ekoros. It was colored, he had heard, with magical salts thrown into the flames.

He roused Snish to steer again, and trimmed the sail to bear toward it. The wind was still high for such a tack.

The galley heeled dangerously, and Snish grew ill again. "We'll never touch land alive," gasped the little wizard. "The wind is crowding us on the rocks!" His whine became a warning shriek. "Captain—ahead!"

Theseus saw the glint of that far light upon leaping spray. He heard the thunder of wild water, and ran toward the steering oars. But the galley plunged upon the rocks. Fangs of stone bit through the hull, water foamed into the empty oarsmen's pit. Rigging snapped. The mast splintered, smashed down.

An instant of silence followed the crash, and: "Captain, it is the spell that follows me!" wailed Snish. "No ship that I am aboard ever comes safe to port!"

The galley listed dangerously as the wave ebbed. The next foamed over the stern, and Theseus thought that they were going to sink. But the crest lifted the ship, drove it between two great rocks.

The hull lodged there. The higher waves poured over it, and filled the pit. Loosening timbers groaned to the battering of the sea. Soon, Theseus knew, they would break apart. He peered to left of the far changing beacon, seeking the shadow of land.

Dawn presently revealed the hills of Crete, dark with cypress forests, marching across the south. Theseus cut loose a broken spar, knotted hand ropes to it, and rolled it over the side. Snish protested that he feared the water and had never learned to swim. Theseus dragged him from the wreck, towed him sputtering to the floating yard. The wind drifted them shoreward.

Peering back northward, Theseus saw the sun's rays pick out scattered black sails, tiny and distant. "The fleet!" he muttered. "Phaistro will soon be after us again."

The squat little wizard sat uneasily astride the drifting spar, and one brown arm—which still glittered with the green jade bracelets of Tai Leng—made an apprehensive gesture toward the shore.

"Phaistro's fleet is nothing," he croaked. "The real danger lies ahead. For Talos, the giant of brass, patrols the coasts of Crete." The croak became a breathless whisper. "Captain—look!"

Far away toward Knossos, between the blue of the sea and the rising green of the hills, Theseus thought he saw a glancing flash that had the color of brass.

SEVEN

SNISH SLID fearfully off the spar into the sea. His squat brown body was shivering with cold and fear, his huge yellow eyes bulging out.

"My soul!" wheezed the little wizard. "My naked, helpless soul! Why did I let fate drive me out of peaceful Babylon? Captain Firebrand, we are doomed!"

"Don't drown yourself!" Theseus laughed, just a little uneasily. "That gleam was far off. Perhaps it was only the sun on some housewife's well-scoured pot."

Snish clung trembling to the ropes.

"I am wizard enough to know the sight of Talos," he croaked anxiously. "The brass man is fleet enough to patrol all the coasts of Crete from sunrise to sunset. And wizardry guides his eyes, so no intruders can escape him.

"Oh, if I had stayed a cobbler in far Babylon!"

He pulled himself up beside the spar, and his popping yellow eyes peered over it for a moment toward the shore. But nothing moved there, and he slipped back into the sea.

"I was a cobbler in Babylon," he wheezed. "But Babylon is an old city. Its empire has crumbled, and all its greatness is but a haunting memory. The caravans pass it by. And business is terrible."

He sighed. "Even the wizards in Babylon are poor, for they have no such power as the warlocks of Crete. There was one whose boots I patched for seven years, and he was never rich enough to pay even a copper bit upon his bill.

"It was he who taught me the small arts of wizardry that I know. One day when he brought his boots to be soled, I told him I had no leather and no money. He offered to teach me all his sorcery, if I would only sole the boots. And I did. But I had better remained a cobbler!" His hand quivered on the ropes. "For wizardry made me an exile from my own Babylon." His voice was a nasal sob. "It cursed me with this perversity of the elements. And now it is bringing the monster Talos down upon me!"

"But you are still a wizard!" Theseus was intently watching the dark shoreline, shading his eyes for another warning glint of brass. "And now I am going to call upon your wizardry. The Cretans have been warned that Captain Firebrand is destined to victory in the games, and all the fleet is hunting for him. But they know nothing of Gothung the Northman, who is the Gamecock's steersman. You saw him—a square-headed giant, with long yellow hair."

"Snish, give me Gothung's likeness!"

Waiting for the change, Theseus looked down at the little brown man shivering in the water. His sword belt began to feel uncomfortable, and he automatically let it out. A heavy strand of hair fell across his face. He saw that it was straw-yellow.

"It is done, Captain Firebrand," the little wizard wheezed. "But remember—the spell is feeble. A close touch—even a kiss—will make you the hunted pirate again."

Theseus was staring at his hands. They were not the lean hands he knew, but huge as hams, sun-reddened, freckle-splotched, covered with white-bleached hair.

"Forget Captain Firebrand," he whispered. "I am Gothung the Northman—a simple mariner, wrecked on the coast of Crete." He looked down at Snish. "But what of your own guise?"

The little wizard sank lower in the water.

"Not in Crete!" he croaked. "The warlocks of Knossos are too many and too jealous. The peculiar welcome they reserve for visiting wizards is famous, even to Babylon." His teeth chattered. "And it is a ghastly thing! No, I am just the poor cobbler, Snish. And I shall attempt no sorcery, master, save what you demand of me."

The wind had carried them on toward the shore. The beach was no more than an arrow-flight ahead, when Snish pulled himself up beside the yard again, and his yellow face went lax with dread.

"Captain Gothung!" he wheezed faintly. "It is Talos—coming around the headland!"

The little wizard had professed an inability to swim. But now he caught his breath and released the ropes and dived with the skill of an otter. The spar drifted on. Theseus watched the wooded point. And a gleaming metal giant came stalking into view, and waded out through the breakers.

Talos stood twice the height of a man. The metal of his huge body seemed pliant, living; the bright skin flexed as he moved. And the waves that struck his mighty legs hissed away in steam, so that Theseus knew he must have been uncommonly hot from his race to meet them.

"Man," a vast brazen voice reverberated across the surf, "who are you?"

The eyes of Talos were like holes into a furnace; their yellow glare was blinding. His immense bright face reflected a simple and terrible strength—a strength, Theseus thought, that lay chiefly in his metal thews. With the water bursting into white steam about his naked middle, he waited ahead of the spar.

Theseus looked again for Snish, and began to suspect that the little wizard had transformed himself into a fish. He cupped hands to his lips, and shouted back across the surf: "I am just a simple mariner, trying to reach land from the wreck yonder."

The burning eyes looked past him, toward the rocks, and the mighty voice of Talos boomed: "What ship is that?"

"That was a pirate," Theseus told him. "The magical wind of Minos drove it on the breakers last night. I was a prisoner, chained to the oars. I cried out to Minos and the Dark One, and they spared my life."

The fiery eyes of Talos came back to him. "Who was captain of the pirates?"

"He is a lean tall Achean, with red hair."

"Was his name Firebrand?"

47

"The pirates," said Theseus, "called him Captain Firebrand."

"Captain Firebrand!" The voice of Talos was like thunder. "Where is he now?"

"He lies on the wreck," shouted Theseus. "He was wounded in a battle with the fleet, and most of the pirates slain. He was running before the storm, to escape, when the ship went on the rocks. The mast fell across his legs, and pinned him to the deck. He cursed me, when I left him, and mocked the names of Minos and the Dark One."

Talos waded forward, with the water hissing higher about his bright hot body.

"That is his last folly," rolled the brazen voice. "For Minos knew that the pirate would approach this coast last night, and he sent me to destroy him."

The brass man abruptly halted, and his flaming eyes flashed cunningly.

"Talos is no fool," he boomed. "Are you not one of the pirates yourself, seeking to escape before the admiral takes you for the games or the Dark One?"

"Ask Captain Firebrand," advised Theseus, "when you find him."

"I shall ask him," roared the brass man, "before I pick the limbs from his body. And if you have lied to me you won't escape. For, mark you, Talos is no fool!"

He waded past the spar. The waves came hissing up over his shoulders. They made white steam about his head, and covered him. Briefly his bright head came up again, as he crossed a bar, and once more vanished.

The spar touched gravel. Theseus splashed ashore. He looked back, wondering what had become of Snish. The little wizard popped out of the water and came stumbling up the beach. His seamed face was blue, and he sobbed painfully for breath.

"Splendid, Gothung!" he gasped. "You lie like a Cretan, already. But I thought I would drown before the brass man passed. Let's get out of sight before he returns."

They crossed a wide dusty trail, where enormous prints of metal feet were spaced three yards apart, and started climbing up the steep forested hill beyond. Theseus broke the way, and the short-legged wizard fell panting behind.

Presently a distant brazen reverberation reached Theseus, and there was a far-off crashing among the trees.

With a miraculous second wind, Snish overtook him. "Our brazen friend," he wheezed, grinning, "who is no fool!"

But Talos did not overtake them, and presently Theseus and his companion crossed the wooded summit and came into view of the valley beyond. Flocks grazed on grassy slopes. Low hills were green with vines and olives, and a stream, below, wandered through fields of wheat and barley. The bright-walled houses of a distant village peered through the groves.

"A beautiful land!" sighed Snish. "It is as fair as the plain about my own far-off Babylon."

"It is a beautiful land." The voice of Theseus was grim. "Its beauty slumbers, fast in the bonds of an evil wizardry. But we have come to set it free!"

They went on down into the valley. Snish begged Theseus to leave the Falling Star hidden beside the way. The sword was too splendid, he said, to be carried by any common shipwrecked mariner; it would betray them.

Theseus would not abandon the weapon. But he wound the inlaid hilt with a rawhide thong, to disguise it, and stained the bright blade with soot.

A shepherd gave them a breakfast of barley cakes and ripe cheese and sour wine. When they reached the village, Snish found the chief merchant of the place, and sold one of his green jade bracelets for a handful of silver shekels.

From the village they followed the westward road, toward Knossos. It was a good, stone-paved way. Trains of laden donkeys plodded along it, and sometimes they met a noble in chariot or palanquin.

As the wandering Northman, Theseus spoke to the travelers they met and the peasants toiling in their little fields and vineyards by the way. He found them a busy, pleasant folk; yet all of them were haunted, it seemed to him, with an unceasing dread of the dark powers that ruled Crete.

Terror came into their eyes when a Minoan priest went by, carried by silent slaves in a black-curtained litter. The blue pinch of hunger was on many faces, and some spoke hopelessly of crushing tithes and taxes. All the young folk hid, when a file of black lancers passed, lest they be seized to perish in the games at Knossos.

That night Theseus and the yellow wizard reached the highway that ran southward from Ekoros to Bandos, the

49

second city of Crete, whose revenues were enjoyed by the noble Phaistro. They slept at an inn on the highway.

When they came out of the tavern, next morning, Snish gulped and stared at a notice that a scribe was painting on the plastered wall. The scribe signed it with the double ax of Minos, and Theseus read:

A reward of twenty talents of silver will be paid from the imperial treasury for the head of a certain Achean pirate, called the Firebrand, who was recently cast on the shore of Crete. The guild of magicians, in addition, offers half a talent of silver for the head of a minor Babylonian wizard, believed to be with the pirate.

Snish had turned a pallid green. Theseus caught his trembling arm, and led him out of the little circle of staring pack drivers and peasants, and down the road toward Knossos.

EIGHT

KNOSSOS, the dwelling of Minos, was itself a city. The greatest and oldest and most splendid palace in the world, it stood upon a low eminence beside the Kairatos River, three miles above the harbor town. Built and rebuilt for a thousand years, it covered six acres, and its mass rose five stories above the long central court. The wonders of it were known in every land, and the guarded magazines beneath it were rumored to hold the greatest treasure hoard ever gathered.

To seaward of Knossos lay the city of Ekoros, which was the metropolis of Crete. Scattered all about upon the low hills were the villas of the nobles, the great merchants, and the more powerful magicians, their gay-painted walls gleaming through groves of palms and olives.

The harbor town, below Ekoros, walled the river's mouth with docks and warehouses. There lay the trading ships that sailed to Egypt and Troy and Mycenae and Tiryns and a hundred other coasts, to carry wine and oil and purple cloth and bronze tools and the graceful pottery of Crete, to bring back silver and gold and amber and tin and furs from the north, copper and murex-purple from the islands, papyrus and incense and grain from Egypt, even silk and jade and pearls from the far-off east.

Theseus and Snish paused for a time where the road topped a hill, looking across at the vast rambling maze of the palace, and the crowded houses of sprawling Ekoros, and the busy shipping in the harbor beyond. At the outskirts of the city, below the palace, they could look down into a long oval bowl whose sides were tiers of seats.

"That must be the place of the games," whispered Theseus. "I shall fight there. And, when I have won, all this will be mine!" He made a broad gesture, over the palace and the city and the harbor, and out toward the sea. "And the reign of the warlocks and the Dark One will be ended."

"Easy words," returned the cynical nasal voice of Snish. "But the doing will take more." His frog-face grinned. "How are you going to get into the games?"

"They are open to any who would challenge the reign of Minos."

"But none ever do," said Snish. "Now Minos is searching for Captain Firebrand, because he has a prescience of what might happen in the games. If you volunteer to fight, it will take no wizard to penetrate the guise of Gothung!"

Theseus tugged at the wide thick brush of his yellow beard.

"Then I'll not volunteer."

A woodcutter overtook them, driving two donkeys laden with faggots. They spoke a little with him, asking the questions that strangers would ask, and presently he pointed out a grove of olives upon a low hill.

"That is a sacred grove," he told them. "In the midst of it is a little temple, that covers the most ancient shrine in Crete." His voice lowered, and his gnarled fingers made a quick propitiatory gesture. "For it is there that the womb of the Earth-Mother opened, and Cybele came forth in her human likeness to be the mother of mankind."

His short whip cut viciously across the nearest donkey's rump.

"I have seen Ariadne," he boasted. "With her dove and her serpent, she comes to the shrine in a white-curtained palan-

51

quin." He cut at the other donkey's belly. "Ariadne is the daughter of Minos, and the vessel of Cybele. She is a sorceress, and a goddess, and her beauty is as blinding as the sun."

His brown face twisted into a leer.

"When my wood is sold," he told them, "I will have three drinks of strong wine, and then I am going to the temple of Cybele." He grinned, and his cracking whip brought blood from the nearest donkey's flank. "Three drinks of wine, and any temple slut becomes as beautiful as Ariadne."

Theseus nodded at the panting Snish, and they strode ahead again.

"Perhaps Ariadne is a goddess," he said softly. "But, nevertheless, she is going to be mine—for she is part of the prize that belongs to the victor in the games."

"Or a part of the bait," croaked Snish, "that the warlocks use to lure men into the arms of death!"

They crossed a stone bridge, and came into Ekoros. This was the poor section of the city, where dwelt the lesser artisans, small shopkeepers, and laborers from the docks. Flimsy buildings, three stories high, confined a powerful stench to the five-foot street.

Most of the street was a foul, brown mud, the rest a shallow open sewer in which a thin trickle of yellow slime ran through piles of decaying garbage and reeking manure. Flies made a dark cloud above the ditch, and their buzzing was an endless weary sound.

Gaunt women trudged through the mud with jars of water on their heads. Screaming hucksters carried little trays of fruits and cakes, brown with crawling flies. Blind beggars screamed for alms. Slatternly dark women screamed conversations out of windows and doorways. Naked brown babies, standing in the mud, screamed for no visible reason at all.

Or perhaps, Theseus guessed from their bloated bellies and pinched cheeks, they were hungry.

"Crete is a splended empire." His voice rang hard above the shrieking din. "Knossos is the most splendid building on earth, crammed with treasures of art. The nobles and the merchants and the warlocks lounge in their green-shaded villas. But these are the people of Crete!"

"And a foul lot they are!" Snish held his nose. "They make even the slums of Babylon smell like a garden in bloom. We have money; let's get on to a better quarter."

He quickened his pace, but Theseus stopped him.

"Give me the money."

Reluctantly, Snish surrendered the little handful of tiny dump-shaped silver shekels. Theseus began buying the stocks of astonished hucksters, passing out dates and honey cakes to beggars and shrieking children. Intelligence of this incredible bounty spread swiftly, and soon the narrow street was packed. Snish tugged fearfully at the arm of Theseus.

"Caution, Gothung!" he croaked faintly. "Men with prices on their heads should not gather mobs about them. Come—"

A horn snarled, and his voice died. A hush fell upon the street, disturbed only by gasps and fearful murmurs. The silent mob began to melt past corners and into doorways. A woman slipped to the side of Theseus.

"Come with me," she whispered. "Hide in my room until the Etruscan guards are gone. I want a strong, brave man again. Once I was in the temple of Cybele. But the high priestess turned me out, because men said that I was more beautiful than Ariadne!"

Theseus looked at her. She was bent a little, and the white-powdered shoulders revealed by her open bodice were thin with years; the rouged face was hollow-eyed and haggard.

"Here is money." He dropped the rest of the rough silver coins into her lean hand. "But I am seeking Ariadne herself."

"You think I am too old." Bitterness cracked her voice, and her fingers closed like brown claws on the silver. "But Ariadne is ten times my age, and more! It is only sorcery that gives her the look of youth and beauty." She tugged at his arm. "But come," she urged, "before the goddess overhears our blasphemy. For here she is!"

Then the horn sounded again. The woman fled, lifting her flounced skirt from the splashing mud. Magically, the street had cleared. There was only a lame, naked child, that the rush had pushed into the gutter. It tried to run, fell, lay still, as if too frightened even to scream.

"Come, Gothung!" The voice of Snish was a husky rasp, and his face had turned yellow-green. "This street is no place for us."

Theseus shrugged off his clutching arm, strode back toward the silently sobbing child. But the horn blared again, and two black stallions came prancing around a bend in the street.

They filled the narrow way, and the bronze greaves of their riders brushed against the walls on either side.

"Make way!" an angry voice barked above the jingle of spurs and bits. "Make way for the white palanquin of Ariadne!"

"Run!" Snish overtook Theseus. "The Etruscans—"

"But the child!"

Theseus ran back, toward the brown, naked infant, lying petrified with fear on the edge of the gutter. He was too late. It shrieked once, under the great hoofs, and lay still again.

Trembling, Theseus snatched the bits and stopped the horse. He looked up at the swart, helmeted rider. Dark with anger, the Etruscan dropped the silver horn to its thong, tugged furiously at a long bronze sword.

"Wait," Theseus said softly. "Let the people get out of the way."

"Loose my bits, gutter rat!" roared the Etruscan. "For this outrage, you will be flung into the games."

"Probably," said Theseus. "But there is no haste."

The other horseman, meantime, had cleared his own saber. He swung down with it, savagely, at the bare, magically blond head of Theseus. But Theseus leaned under the neck of the horse he held. And the dark-stained Falling Star, whipping up, slashed the Etruscan's fingers and sent the bronze blade rattling into the gutter.

The wounded Etruscan made a bellow of rage and pain. The other jerked and spurred his mount, attempting to ride down Theseus. But Theseus clung to the bits, swung clear of the pawing hoofs. And the steel sword, with two swift strokes, severed girth and reins.

The saddle slid down the back of the rearing horse. The Etruscan sat down upon it, violently, in the open sewer. There was an unpleasant splash and a louder buzzing of flies. In a moment, however, the man was on his feet, gripping his saber and mouthing soldierly curses.

Theseus released the unsaddled horse, and crouched to meet the Etruscan. But steel had not touched bronze, when a woman's voice, clear and full as a golden bugle, pealed to them:

"Hold! Who halts my guard?"

Theseus saw that a rich palanquin, carried by four sturdy, panting slaves, had come up behind the disarmed horseman.

The white curtains were drawn open, and its occupant was sitting up on her couch, to look out.

Ariadne!

Ariadne of the white doves, sorceress of the serpent! The woman in the palanquin, Theseus knew, could be no other. Daughter of Minos, and divine vessel of the All-Mother, Cybele.

"Who dares halt Ariadne?"

Her proud voice was a golden melody. It touched an eager chord in the heart of Theseus, and he stood with wide eyes drinking in her loveliness.

Her skin was white, white as the dove on her smooth, bare shoulder. Her full lips were red as hot blood, her eyes green and cold as ice. And the hair that foamed about her shoulders was a flaming splendor.

Her hair was red, redder than the locks of Captain Firebrand had been. Soft lights rippled and flowed in the thick wavy masses of it. It was a cascade of shining glory, falling over her long, white body.

Theseus struggled for breath. He had sworn to win Ariadne, as a trophy of victory in the games. Now he made a hot renewal of the oath. He saw that she was worth all the storied wealth of Knossos, that her beauty was a power vast as the wizardry of Crete.

Briefly, Theseus wondered if she were as old as the woman of the street had said, and he saw a confirming shadow of wisdom and weariness in her cold, green eyes. And he thought that none but a goddess could ever have been so beautiful.

A gasping curse brought him back to himself, and he found the unhorsed Etruscan close upon him. He crouched, and the Falling Star flashed out to parry the long bronze saber.

"Stop!" Ariadne's golden voice pealed out again. "Let him speak." The cool, green eyes surveyed Theseus haughtily. "The savage is clever with his blade. Ask him his name, and what he seeks in Crete."

"I have ears." Theseus rang his steel defiantly against the saber. "Tell her that I am Gothung, a wanderer from the north. Tell her that I came to Crete to hire my sword to Minos. But say that, having seen the people of Crete, I would fight for them instead."

Her splendid head tossed angrily, and she shouted:

"Call another detachment, and take the insolent Northman!"

Nursing bleeding fingers, the mounted man spurred his horse down the street. The one on foot came at Theseus, with bronze saber upflung. But the steel blade turned the stroke, a swift slash opened his arm to tendon and bone, and the saber dropped in the mud.

Theseus leaped forward, menaced the palanquin slaves.

"Set down the litter," he commanded.

At the point of red-dripping steel, they obeyed. Theseus ripped aside the white linen curtains, and looked in upon Ariadne. Clad in a flounced green gown, her long white body sprawled lazily on the cushions. Her cool green eyes met the hot eyes of Theseus, without hint of fear.

"When my rider comes back with aid, Northman," she said softly, "you will regret your insolence to a goddess."

"Meantime, I am the master." The flat voice of Theseus was equally soft. "And the All-Mother should display compassion. Get out." His red sword gestured. "Pick the dead child up out of the gutter."

She lay still, and the green eyes turned frosty.

"No man would dare!" she whispered.

The palanquin slaves gasped mutely as Theseus shifted the sword, and reached his red-dripping hand through the curtains. Her white arm went angrily tense under his fingers, but he dragged her out into the muddy street.

"Northman!" Her quivering words were almost soundless. "For this, you shall feed the Dark One!"

"Perhaps," said Theseus. "But pick up the body."

Tall, defiant, the red handprint bright on her skin, she made no move. Theseus shoved. She went sprawling sidewise into the sewer, thrust white hands into its reeking muck to check her fall.

Breathless, silent, she got slowly back to her feet. Flies swarmed dark about her, filth dripped from her hands and her gown. She tried to scramble out of the ditch. Theseus met her with his red steel.

"The child," he said, "All-Mother!"

For a moment her green eyes stared at him. They had turned dark, and something glittered in their frosty depths. Her dripping hands clenched, and slowly relaxed. Silently, then, she bent and lifted the small, brown body in her arms.

Theseus caught her elbow, helped her back to the palanquin.

"Thus, Cybele," he whispered, "you have begun to prove your motherhood. But the proof is not done, and we shall meet again when the games are played."

The red lips moved, but she spoke no word.

Another horn snarled, and the drum of hoofs and the rattle of weapons came down the narrow street. Gripping the Falling Star, Theseus turned away from the white palanquin. He glimpsed the pallid face of Snish, peering furtively from the doorway of a wine shop.

"Well, cobbler," he shouted, "there was no need to volunteer!"

NINE

THESEUS MADE a necessary gesture toward his own defense. In fact, the Etruscans being the fighting men they were, he was able to make the gesture quite vigorous, with no danger of escape.

An officer in a chariot whose axle spanned the street, was followed by a dozen men on foot. He left the chariot at the corner, with a slave to hold the horses, and led six men up the street. The others vanished, and Theseus guessed that they were going around the block to take him from behind.

A dozen alleys and doorways beckoned, but he brushed the humming flies off his red hands, and waited quietly. Three tall, notched shields made a moving barrier, from wall to wall, and long bronze blades lifted through the notches.

Waiting, Theseus snatched another glimpse of Ariadne. One of the palanquin slaves stood ready to assist her back into the litter. But she was standing in the mud beside it, the child's brown body, dripping blood and filth, still clutched against her. Her green eyes were fixed on Theseus.

"Wait, slave!" Theseus caught her muted golden voice. "Let me see the Northman fight."

He fought. The Falling Star was thin and keen enough to probe far through the bull-hide shields, and the narrow slippery way hampered the rigid formation of the Etruscans. One man, and then another, slipped down behind the wall of shields.

If he had really sought escape, Theseus knew, he could have leaped through the wall when it wavered. But he waited for men to replace the fallen, waited for the second wall to form behind him. And he heard the ring of Ariadne's voice: "Take the savage alive, for the games!"

The probing steel found a heart behind the second barrier. But the walls came inexorably together. Bronze blades reached Theseus, from before and behind. But it was a mace that reached over the rawhide wall, and crushed him out of consciousness.

With bitter mouth and splitting head, Theseus came back to life in a dungeon whose fetor was thicker than the street's. This was a square pit, twenty feet deep. The walls were polished, well-fitted stone, unscalable. A faint, gray light came through a grating in the roof.

Dimly, that light revealed his five companions, groaning or snoring on the bare stone floor. They were all condemned criminals, he learned, waiting for the games. A slave who had been indiscreet with his master's wife. A palace scullion who had got drunk and burned a roast. An unemployed carpenter who had stolen bread. Two merchants who had neglected to pay certain tithes to the Dark One. They were all hopeless as men already dead.

The pit was not a pleasant place. Water trickled down the walls, to make foul little pools on the porous gypsum floor. Sanitary arrangements did not exist. Molded bread and rotten meat were dropped at uncertain intervals through the grate. Time was marked by the daily fading of that faint, gray light.

Days dragged by, and Theseus knew that bad food and exposure were sapping even the rugged strength of Gothung. His body was stiff and ulcerated from sleeping on the foul wet stone, and monotony numbed his mind.

To fill the days, he began speculating upon the possibility of escape—even though this hard imprisonment was a thing that he had risked his life to gain.

"It can't be done," the scullion assured him. "In three hundred years, no man has escaped from the dungeons of Minos. We are stripped. We are not thrown even a bone, to serve as weapon or tool. The walls are strong masonry, and there is only living rock behind them. Only a fly could climb to the roof. And nothing much larger could pass through that bronze grate—which is locked with a wizard's secret."

"Still," Theseus insisted, "I believe I could escape even from such a pit as this—if it had to be done!"

They counted the days, until the moon of Minos, when the games would be observed. No word was spoken to them through the grate. Even when the carpenter died, after days of coughing, the guards ignored their calls. The body crumbled into a pool of decay.

The day arrived at last, the grate was unlocked, and lassos hissed down and caught them one by one. Theseus stood waiting under the door, while the others crouched moaning with dread in the corners, but he was the last taken.

The rope whipped under his arms, hauled him upward. Black-mantled Minoan priests dragged him down a dark stone corridor. A door opened, to make a square of dazzling light. Lances prodded him, and he walked out into blinding sun.

The dry heat was good to his naked body, stiff as it was from his wet stone bed, and caked with filth. The clean air was precious. For a moment it seemed enough to be out of the pit, and he forgot that this must be the moment for which he had planned and fought and endured the dungeon.

Weak from hunger and hardship, he stood swaying in the sun. It was a little time before he could see anything. But he felt hot, dry sand under his feet, and heard the deep-throated murmur of a great crowd. Somewhere a bull was bellowing. And his nostrils caught the faint sweet odor of blood.

Abruptly, behind him, bronze horns made a strident fanfare, and a harsh-voiced herald began a monotonous chant:

"This man, called Gothung the Northman, now enters the sacred cyclic games, to seek the throne of Minos. Therefore let him be faced with the nine trials, to test the will of the Dark One in his three aspects.

"For the Dark One is a deity of three aspects, bull and man and god. And if all the aspects of the Dark One shall favor the candidacy of this man, then he shall be seated upon the sacred throne of Minos, and wed to the All-Mother, Cybele, who dwells in Ariadne the daughter of Minos, and shall reign over all Crete as regent of the Dark One. And Minos shall go into the Labyrinth to meet the deity who has disowned him.

"But if the Dark One fails to show favor to this man, in any aspect, then he shall die, and his carcass shall be flung into the Labyrinth so that the Dark One may feast upon his craven soul."

By the time that the herald was done, Theseus could see. This was the same oval bowl that he and Snish had marked from the hill. Blood splotched the blinding white sand that spread the long arena. The seats above the curving wall were crowded with the upper tenth of the hundred thousand of Ekoros.

Apprehensively, Theseus searched for the gleaming brazen bulk of Talos. For the brass giant, having met him as he came ashore and listened to the lie about Captain Firebrand, might—if he really were no fool—penetrate the guise of Gothung. But Talos was not in sight.

Hopefully, then, Theseus looked for Snish. Since the little wizard had not come to share his dungeon, Theseus believed that he must have escaped, might be useful again. But Snish, he knew, had courage for no real risk. He was not surprised when he failed to discover the little Babylonian.

Above the center of the arena he found a section of curtained boxes, and glimpsed faces that he knew. He saw the sallow, hawk-nosed visage of Amur the Hittite, and the thin, dark face of Admiral Phaistro. He even caught the husky, excited voice of the Hittite:

"Half a talent, that the first bull kills the Northman!"

Flashing past them, the eyes of Theseus found Ariadne. She sat apart, in a white-curtained box. A white dove rested on her bare white shoulder. Her green gown heightened the green of her eyes.

She was watching him, fixedly. A curious, eager smile touched her smooth, white face. Her flaming head made a lazy little nod, as if of satisfaction. Her smooth arm beckoned to one of the busy slaves, bearing the yellow arm bands of Amur, who were taking wagers.

"Three talents," she called softly, "that the Northman dies in the first three trials."

Theseus dragged his eyes, with an effort, away from her haunting and insolent beauty. He found a black-curtained box beyond her. And his heart checked when he knew that he looked at last upon the dreaded warlock who had ruled Crete for twenty generations.

Curiously, Minos looked like neither wizard nor king. He was a short, fat man, and the hands folded in the lap of his white silk robe were short-fingered, plump, pink, and dimpled. His face was round and red and dimpled, too, his eyes small and blue and merry. Perfectly white, fine as a woman's, his hair was long and daintily dressed. His pink, plump arms were laden with silver bracelets.

Theseus stared again. For this looked like the sort of man who would keep a tiny shop, and be always poor from giving dates and honey cakes to children. He didn't look like the wizard-god who held half the world in cruel subjection. But he was.

Then something moved in the rear of the curtained box, and Theseus saw another figure. A gaunt, stooped man, all in black, with a seamed, shrunken face that was like dark wax, and hollow, flaming eyes. The cadaverous face, the whole dark-swathed frame, carried an impression of leering, sinister power. Here was one who looked like a warlock, and doubtless was. For this, Theseus guessed, was the dreaded and infamous Daedalus.

The two spoke briefly in the box. Theseus heard their voices. That of Minos was soft and limpid as a woman's, silver-sweet. The tones of the other were sepulchral, with a cold, rasping harshness that set Theseus to shivering.

They used the secret priestly tongue, so that Theseus could not understand. But in a moment Minos beckoned to one of the slaves, and the woman-voice said softly:

"Nine talents on the Northman—one that he wins each game!"

Then Theseus shuddered indeed. Had these warlocks already pierced his guise? Were they merely playing a game? Else why did Minos calmly wager on the loss of his empire? Theseus searched that genial dimpled face. The small blue eyes of Minos twinkled back at him merrily.

TEN

SILVER HORNS snarled again, at the lips of three black-robed priests. And the harsh voice of the herald rang once more across the sun-flooded, hushed arena:

"First let the challenger test the will of the Dark One in his aspect of the bull. The first three steps are three wild bulls

61

from Thessaly, and their horns will show the Dark One's will."

Bull-leaping, Theseus knew from the tales he had heard, was the dangerous national sport of Crete. The performers, usually slaves or captives, required years of training. Often, on less solemn occasions, this same arena must have been devoted to that sport.

A dark passage opened in the end of the arena, and a great black bull lumbered out upon the blinding white sand. Its mighty head was flung high, and the sun gleamed on its cruel polished horns.

Standing naked on the hot sand, Theseus found time to recall Cretan paintings that showed bull-vaulting scenes. The daring acrobat seized the horns of the charging bull, to be lifted gracefully over the animal. He wished briefly that he had been trained in that perilous art, but he had not.

The bull stopped, stood for a moment as if bewildered by the walls and the watching thousands. Its bellow was a deep, ominous sound. It pawed up a cloud of sand, dropped its horns to gore the earth.

Then its eyes discovered the lone straight figure of Theseus, and it charged. Theseus waited, motionless. His senses seemed queerly sharpened. He felt the dry hot grains of sand under the bare soles of his feet, and the sting of the sun, and the sticky legs of a fly crawling up his abdomen.

Time seemed oddly slowed. He felt aware of every watching eye, and found time even for a glance toward Ariadne. She was leaning forward in the white-curtained box, white face intent, cool green eyes fixed on him. He thought of her wager that the bulls would kill him, and shouted a taunt at her:

"All-Mother, remember your child!"

There was no time to see her response, however, for the bull was upon him. He caught his breath, and set his feet in the hot sand, and tensed the great lean body of Gothung. He wished that he were not so stiff and weak from the dungeon, for the thing he had to do required a quick, smooth-flowing strength.

Theseus was untrained in bull-vaulting. But he had traveled through Thessaly. He had seen the half-savage Thessalonian herdsmen seize a charging bull by the horns, and throw it with a clever twist. He had even tried the thing himself.

It took but half a heartbeat. The wide-spaced grasp upon

the curving horns. The twist aside. The sudden thrust of all his weight upon the leverage of the horns. But he had never thrown such a mighty beast as this.

Under the hot black skin, tremendous muscles resisted. The horns surged up, to toss him. Every thew of tall Gothung's body was strained. But the huge head twisted aside. The weight of the bull finished the thing, and the very momentum of the charge. The animal went down in a kicking pile,

Theseus walked out of the little cloud of dust, and breathed again. His limbs were trembling. In spite of the sun, a quick sweat made him a little cold. Standing relaxed, watching the bull, he caught voices from the vast murmur of the crowd:

"But he can't threw three!" . . . "See, he is weak and shaking already!" . . . "Ten to one the first man kills him, if he escapes the bulls." . . . "No man has won in a thousand years!" . . . "No man will ever win!"

The bull struggled back to its feet. It stood with lowered head, bellowing and pawing up sand. But it did not charge again. Presently the horns blared, and the herald shouted:

"Gothung the Northman has survived the first test, by the Dark One in his aspect of the bull. Gothung has mounted one step toward the throne of Minos. Therefore let him try the second step."

A wide gate was opened at the arena's farther end. Light-footed professional bull-vaulters, with their red mantles, lured the first bull through it. The gate was closed, and the second admitted.

The second bull refused to fight. If Theseus had run, it might have pursued him. But he stood still in the center of the arena, weak with hunger and the strain of his first contest, while the animal ran around and around the wall, seeking escape.

The thousands jeered it. The bull-vaulters hurled barbed javelins into its black hide in an effort to infuriate it. But it merely ran the faster, and at last leaped over the gate and escaped from the arena.

The third, however, was made of more deadly stuff. It lowered its head without a sound, and came with a savage rush at Theseus. Theseus crouched again, and spread his hands to grasp the horns.

But they twisted, evaded his fingers. The bull swerved. The horns made a vicious slash. A keen point raked across the ribs of Theseus. Pain staggered him. He stood swaying as the bull wheeled beyond him, came back. Again the horns escaped his hands, caught his thigh.

The beast wheeled and charged again. This time he knew its way. His hands were waiting, and that quick deceptive twist brought the horns into them. He flung all his strength, not against the savage thrust of that mighty head, but with it. The bull went down. One horn plowed deep into the sand, and the head turned back under the body. There was the sharp little crack of a snapping spine, and it lay still.

Theseus swayed aside, quivering from the effort, gasping for breath. The sun was driving, merciless. The white sand began to move in slow undulations under him, like a sea of white fire. The red marks the horns had left on chest and thigh were dully painful, and flies sought them.

A deep awed whisper had come from the mob on the piled tiers of seats. Now, reeling, Theseus listened to the talk as the bets were laid again. The boxes were close above him. Without looking, he knew the golden voice of Ariadne:

"Three more talents, that the men kill him!"

"Taken, daughter." It was the silken voice of Minos himself. "Three talents that he lives to face the gods."

Theseus shuddered, and covered his eyes against the searing sun. Was his guise in vain? Was his victory in the games already anticipated—and provided against—by this fat, dimpled, merry-eyed man whose sinister magic had ruled Crete for ten centuries?

The horns made a thin far sound, and the herald's voice seemed to waver and fade upon the hot air:

"The bull is dead. In the aspect of the bull, the Dark One looks with favor upon the candidacy of Gothung the Northman. He has mounted three steps toward the throne of Minos. Now let him test the will of the Dark One in his aspect of the man."

A yoke of black oxen dragged the dead bull out of the arena. Theseus waited, giddy with the heat. His mouth was bitter and dry. It was no great wonder, he reflected, that no man had won these games in a thousand years. The bugles whined again, and a dark Nubian boxer came into the arena.

The man was gigantic, naked but for tight belt and loincloth, long muscles gliding beautifully under oiled gleaming skin. A heavy, leathern helmet protected his head. His hands were heavy with copper-weighted leather cesti—cruel things, that could crush a skull like an egg.

Theseus stood waiting for him, fighting a silent battle with heat and hunger and fatigue. The Nubian crouched, came in. The deadly fists thrust like rams. One caught the arm of Theseus with a bruising shock. The other grazed his head, with staggering pain.

Bare fists were quicker than the loaded ones, but not quick enough. Theseus struck again for the dark shining body. But the Nubian rolled aside, caught his shoulder with a swinging cestus.

Theseus ducked, feinted, danced away. But he was reeling. He wanted to drop on the hot sand, relax, forget, let the black end this agony. The evil power of Minos no longer mattered to him. He had no desire for the rich plunder of Knossos, nor even Ariadne's white beauty.

But—he mustn't fail!

Somehow, he made himself stand again to face the grinning Nubian. He groped for something through the vagueness of his spinning brain. He found it. A trick he had learned, painfully, from a camel driver who had come with a silk caravan from the east.

He tensed his quivering body, crouched, waited. The Nubian struck again. He caught the dark wrist, ridged with the thongs that held the cestus. He twisted, then, dragging the slick oiled arm over his back. A blow on the neck staggered him. But he kept his grip, lunged, bent.

Twisted sidewise from his feet, the Nubian went spinning over the shoulder of Theseus. Released with a final well-timed fling, he came down upon the helmeted head. There was another small muffled snap in the arena, and the boxer was dead.

Black oxen dragged away the body. Horns snarled, and the herald cried:

"Gothung has mounted the fourth step. Let him strive again, with the aspect of the Dark One that is man."

There was a murmur in the crowd. Giddy, reeling, breathless, Theseus did not look up. But he caught the lowered husky voice of Amur the Hittite:

"If Minos is betting on the Northman, I am through. An honest man can't wager with wizards! I'll lay you fifty talents that they have already seen the final victory, in their spheres of time!"

65

Theseus shared the same uneasy suspicion. Blinking against the sun, he found the merry blue eyes of Minos again, and wondered what mockery lay beyond their twinkle. He saw Ariadne, impatient and white, with three talents on his death. And again he glimpsed that gnarled dark figure, in the box behind Minos, and caught the glare of sunken, evil eyes. He shivered once more to the feel of cold, supernal power.

The horns whined again, and Theseus waited. Desperately, he wanted a drink of water. He closed his eyes against the glaring sand, and saw the shaded pool in Attica where he had learned so long ago to swim. Flies clustered about the smarting scratches on his chest and thigh, grimy sweat ran down into his eyes. And at last the second man entered the arena.

This was a swart, little Cretan marine, with his weighted net and bronze-pronged trident. He trotted out watchfully across the sand, spinning the net into a blurring circle. Theseus wished for the good hilt of the Falling Star in his hand, and flexed his empty fingers.

The Cretan circled him cautiously, ran in abruptly, flung the net. But Theseus, watching his narrowed dark eyes, had seen warning of the effort. He crouched, reached out, caught the spinning web.

Once, on Captain Firebrand's pirate galley, a captured marine had paid for his life with instruction in all the tricks of net play. Theseus dropped to his knees upon the sand. But he kept the net spinning, and held its weighted cords from whipping about his limbs, and tossed it back to meet the Cretan.

The marine had lunged after the cast net, with both hands on his trident. The returned net tangled it, tripped him. Theseus caught the trident, dragged it out of clutching hands, reversed it. A bronze point ripped the Cretan's breast and shoulder.

"Do you yield?" Theseus demanded.

White with pain, the man half-lifted himself. Theseus stopped him, with the prongs against his throat. Faintly, then, he gasped:

"I yield."

And he sprawled back on the sand, dead. Theseus dropped the trident and stumbled back from him. He was cold with a shuddering wonderment. He knew that wound had not been fatal.

The horns shrilled. The herald made announcement that the Northman had mounted the fifth step toward the throne

Black oxen returned to drag off the dead marine. Theseus waited, too weary to slap at the flies on his wounds. And at last the third man came into the arena.

This champion of the Dark One was a tall, harsh-visaged Etruscan—one of the wandering warrior race that Minos had brought from the north coasts to guard his throne. Shining bronze plated his helmet and his greaves. He carried a notched shield nearly as tall as himself, and a long bronze sword.

Theseus reeled, staring at the glitter of the sun on that sword. He fought down a brief desire to fling himself upon it, and find a swift, clean end to all his weariness and pain. He brushed the flies away, and fumbled dimly for another plan.

There was a long dark blot on the sand, where the bulls must have killed another victim. That might be useful. Because he had to go on. Not for the throne of Minos, nor the loot of Knossos, nor even Ariadne's insolent beauty. But for a naked brown baby, it seemed, crying in a gutter.

The Etruscan's shield was heavy. Weary as he was, Theseus could move fast enough to keep out of the way for a little time, until he got trapped in a corner. He retreated, turned, paused, fled again.

The Etruscan ran after him, panting, sweating, cursing. The sun was blinding on the helmet and the sword. Theseus passed the dark pool of blood, passed it again, and a third time. But the mercenary avoided it. It was the few drops the dead marine had spilled that set him at last to stumbling.

Theseus stopped, stooped, whirled back. Trembling fingers caught a bronze-greaved leg, lifted. The Etruscan sprawled flat on his back, beneath the long shield. The bare heel of Theseus came down on his elbow, and the bronze sword dropped. Theseus snatched the weapon, swung it high.

But he did not strike.

For Minos, in the black-curtained box, had risen suddenly. His rosy cheeks still dimpled genially, and his small blue eyes were merry. But he lifted a round pink arm, in a gesture of annoyance. A blinding blue bolt whipped out of his empty fingers. Authentic thunder crashed. Smelling of burned leather and seared flesh, the struggling Etruscan fell again.

Eleven

Theseus stood reeling, staring up into those jolly eyes. The dazzling sand rocked again, and the ruddy dimpled smile of Minos was suspended before him like a mask of jovial merriment, against a flaming haze of weariness and pain. He thought that one twinkling eye winked at him, and Minos sat down again.

Despite the sun's dry sting, Theseus felt cold. This thing was proof enough, it seemed to him, that Minos was actually a god, that he in fact commanded the lightning. How, he wondered, was any winner of these contests to make good his claims, against such powers? Was that the meaning of the wink?

Theseus had hoped that the priests and the people would insist on fair play with the winner. But the awed hush that followed that crashing bolt seemed proof enough of Minos' absolute dominion. Theseus could expect no aid.

Few contestants, Theseus guessed, had ever mounted so far toward the throne of Minos. For the seated thousands were leaning forward, breathless, white-faced, staring. Even the voice of the herald had gone hoarse and unsure:

"Gothung the Northman has been favored to mount the throne of Minos, by the Dark One in his aspects of bull and man. Therefore let the Northman now test the will of the Dark One in his sublime aspect of the god."

The horns whined again.

"Gothung will stand and wait at the center of the arena. First let him determine the will of the Dark One through Cybele, daughter of the Dark One and mother of men, whose vessel is the fair Ariadne."

Swaying, bewildered, Theseus stumbled to the middle of the arena. He found the outline of the sacred double ax of Minos, marked with black sand poured upon the white, and stood upon it. Half blinded with the glare of sun on sand, he stood there, watching Ariadne, wondering what the next test would be.

The silver horns sounded again.

Green-eyed Ariadne rose lazily in her white-curtained box. She tossed her head, to send ruddy flame-tresses rippling back, and strolled with an insolent grace out upon a long railed platform that ran before the boxes. The sun turned her long white body to gleaming marble, shimmered green on her daring gown.

The white dove clung to her bare shoulder, fluttering to keep its balance when she moved. The girdle about her thin waist, Theseus saw, was fashioned in the shape of a silver serpent. It seemed to writhe, oddly, as if it were alive— perhaps, Theseus thought, his uncovered head was getting too much sun.

A fat red-robed priestess brought Ariadne a long white bow, and another offered her a full quiver of arrows. Displaying a strength and skill surprising to Theseus, she strung the bow, tested its pull, let the string twang viciously.

Carefully she selected a long, green-feathered arrow from the quiver, nocked it, then stood for a little moment watching Theseus. Her voice rang out, clear as a golden horn:

"Northman, I am glad you have lived to try the steps of the gods. For Cybele has her own quarrel with you."

The drive of the sun was an intolerable searing thrust and Theseus felt a prickling over all his skin, and a weakness in his limbs. His throat was painful and parched, but he managed to shout hoarsely:

"And I have a lesson for Cybele. The All-Mother should not kill, but love."

He saw color, then, in the whiteness of her face. The red splendor of her head made a little angry toss. Slowly, with a splendid strength, she drew the bow, pulled the arrow to her cheek. And her clear voice pealed:

"Even Cybele can slay!"

Something, even in that breathless moment, drew the eyes of Theseus from her tall beauty and her peril. Something made him look high above the curtained boxes. There, in the topmost tier of seats, he glimpsed the face of Snish.

The seamed ugly features of the little Babylonian were stiff and pallid. And his hands came up, with an odd swift gesture, as if to fend the arrow from himself. Could—or would—the little wizard help?

The glance of Theseus fled back to Ariadne. The sun

gleamed on the silver scales of the serpent-girdle, and he thought the bright coils tightened around her. The dove fluttered white wings. And the bow twanged.

Theseus had dodged arrows. He tried to drop flat, at the sound of the string, in hope that the shaft might pass above him. But he couldn't move!

His weary body was held rigid, above that sand-laid outline of the double ax, as if he had been bound to an invisible post. Now he had met the gods—and their wizardry!

But it was an angry defiance that sprang into him, and not a fear. His head set grimly, and his open eyes looked straight to meet the hissing shaft. The warlocks might chain his body, but his mind still fought!

The arrow whispered by his ear!

Free of the invisible bonds, Theseus swayed. A trembling looseness came into his knees, and he wanted to sit down on the burning sand. He shaded his eyes, stared up at the boxes, where an uneasy murmuring ran.

He was incredulous. He could have sworn that the arrow was drawn straight at his right eye. Her practiced stance had told him that Ariadne was a well-skilled archer. Nor could he suspect that, for any possible reason, she had deliberately spared him.

For all color had left her lovely face again. The splendor of her head was high with anger. The green light of her eyes turned dark, dangerous. She turned swiftly to her red-robed priestess, reaching for another arrow.

The soft woman's voice of Minos stopped her.

"Stay, daughter! The Dark One guided your arrow, and it missed. The Northman has mounted the seventh step toward my throne." The small eyes danced genially. "Let him try the eighth."

The dimples deepened as Minos smiled; his fat pink hands made a little gesture to the herald and the priests. Thoroughly puzzled—and still with a deep, invincible apprehension of this stout merry man and his power—Theseus looked up across the silent throng again, and found the wrinkled, wide-mouthed face of Snish.

The yellow popeyes of the little wizard were staring at him. And one of them deliberately winked! Was it Snish, whose arts had deflected the arrow? With a sudden fear that his eyes would betray the Babylonian, Theseus looked swiftly away from him.

The horns keened again, and the herald shouted:

"Now let the Northman test the will of the Dark One through the great Minos, who is his son, and his regent over the earth."

The unseen fetters, Theseus discovered, held his body again, so that he stood unable to move upon the black sign of the double ax. He stood in the blaze of sun, lightheaded, helpless, watching.

Minos stood up, and came out of the black-curtained box, to the platform where Ariadne had stood. For all his plumpness, he moved with a surprising ease and vigor; he almost bounced.

He slipped off the white robe, tossed it to a slave. Bare except for belt and loincloth, his hairless body looked pink and firm. His middle showed evidence of good living, but there was no hint anywhere of a thousand years' decay. His rosy cheeks dimpled to a genial smile, and the small blue eyes twinkled down at Theseus. He might have been the priest of some small deity of wine and song, placing his blessing upon a night of carnival.

"So, Northman, you seek my throne?" Bright laughter bubbled in his woman-voice. "Let the Dark One choose!"

A black-robed priest knelt before him on the platform, offered him with bowed head something long and bent and black. It was a stick of ancient ebony, Theseus saw, curved on one side and flattened on the other, longer than the pink arm of Minos. It was polished to the gleam of glass.

Minos took the boomerang, with a firm and easy grasp. His preliminary swing was strong and free. His pink face smiled like a happy child's, and his blue eyes sparkled warmly. Yet the careful swiftness of his motions convinced Theseus that the eighth test was going to be a very real one.

"O Dark One," he called softly. "Choose!"

With a long and powerful sweep of the round pink arm, he threw the boomerang. Unable to move, Theseus stood on the black emblem of the double ax, watching with defiant level eyes.

For one heartbeat, he knew that it was hurtling straight toward his head. Straight. It was going to hit him. Then, abruptly, making a savage *whi-whi-whi,* it flashed past his head. Another incredible miss!

But a boomerang returns.

Theseus still could not turn his head. But, watching the

faces of the thousands before him, he saw them follow the spinning weapon beyond him, up, back. He heard the hissing whistle of it again.

Heard it, once more, pass him!

It lifted a little puff of white sand before him, danced away like a graceful, live thing, dropped and lay still. Theseus looked up at the rosy face of Minos. It held the same dimpled smile. He waited for a slave to replace the white robe about his shoulders, bounced back into the dark-curtained box.

Horns shrilled again, and the herald croaked:

"The Northman has mounted eight steps toward the throne. Through Minos himself, the Dark One indicates favor. There remains the ninth test. The Northman will learn the final will of the Dark One, through Daedalus the wizard, who is his high priest, his hand, and his voice."

The heart of Theseus was beginning to skip. The blazing white sand spun about him, until he felt that he was floating in a sea of white searing fire. His fatigue was gone. His body was a dead and distant thing; the itch and sting of the flies on his wounds had ceased to matter.

Dimly, he tried to remember what was happening. He had a dim, vague hope that he might escape this final danger, but he couldn't recall what he must do next. He watched Daedalus through a screen of unreality.

The warlock came out of the curtained box, and shed his own black robe. If Minos had looked amazingly young, Daedalus was very old—and yet incredibly strong. His body was dark, hairy, shrunken, gnarled like some ancient tree.

Beneath stringy black hair, his face was creased into wrinkles no few centuries could have wrought. It was waxen, hollow, skeletal. His eyes were deeply sunken, black, flaming with a sinister power. Lean dark claws of fingers raked through his stringy black beard.

While the horns whined again, black-robed priests brought the warlock a leather-thonged sling and a bright, heavy little copper ball. Staring at the ball with those flaming hollow eyes, Daedalus muttered over it, fitted it at last to the socket of the sling.

The sling spun about his head. Hard muscles knotted and quivered, jerking his lean twisted frame swiftly and more swiftly. He was like a dwarfed mountain oak, Theseus thought, battered and shaken in a savage wind. The sling became a blurred wheel of motion. The leather thongs murmured, sighed, screamed.

Theseus found strength again to test his unseen fetters. They held him. But they made no difference now, he thought. For no man could hope to dodge that screaming shot.

It came—whined harmlessly by!

The invisible bonds were abruptly loosed. Theseus pitched to bare knees on the baking white sand, and the whole arena rocked. He saw the baleful malice that twisted the gnarled, evil face of Daedalus, saw him limp angrily back into the dark-curtained box.

Horns shrilled, and the herald stepped forward again. He was pale and perspiring. He tried thrice to speak, gulped thrice for his voice, croaked faintly at last:

"Gothung the Northman has mounted the nine steps to the throne of Minos. In his three aspects, of bull and man and god, the Dark One has shown favor. The tests are done, and Gothung the Northman is chosen to ascend the throne!"

Faint as that voice was, every word rang clear through the brittle tensity of silence that had fallen upon the vast arena. There was a long, intolerable moment of suspension. Swaying on his knees, Theseus watched the bland chubby face of Minos, and his heart was still with dread of another lightning bolt.

But the pink baby-face of Minos dimpled again, his blue eyes shone merrily, and jovial laughter sparked beneath his silken voice:

"Rise, Northman, and take the throne!"

The rosy arm made a little gesture, and Theseus followed it toward the end of the arena. What he saw sent a swift cold tremor through every limb. The massive gate had opened again. Talos, the brazen giant, was striding toward him over the sand.

TWELVE

THESEUS DRAGGED himself once more to his feet, on the black spinning outline of the double ax. His quivering limbs were weak with apprehension of some new and treacherous attack.

But there was nothing, he thought, that he could do against the brass might of Talos.

He waited, feeling the quiver of the sand to the tread of Talos. The twelve-foot shining giant came up to him. The fiery eyes looked down, filled with simple cunning, and the hollow voice rumbled:

"I remember you, Gothung the Northman. I spoke with you when you came ashore from the wrecked galley of the pirate Firebrand." His chuckle was an immense deep reverberation. "And I know you still. For Talos is no fool!"

Theseus felt that Captain Firebrand, just now, was a very dangerous subject. He contrived to stand on the hot sand, swaying. He had no idea what to expect—except fresh peril! The hushed, startled crowd had no look of a people greeting a new ruler. It seemed insane to think that Minos would willingly surrender the throne.

Anxiously, in quest of further aid, his eyes roved up across the tiers of seats, to where he had seen Snish. But the little wizard, as he half expected, had vanished again. If Snish indeed had taken a hand in the games, that was all he could expect. He looked back, with concealed apprehension, into the flame-yellow eyes of Talos.

"Well?" His voice was faint and dry. "What do you want?"

"Master, now you are going to be the new Minos." The words of Talos were a throbbing roll of brazen sound. "And I shall be your slave. I have come to serve you."

"Then," whispered Theseus, "show me the way to the throne I have won."

"Wait, master," rumbled Talos.

A breathless quiet still filled the long bowl. There was not even a whisper, save from Minos and Daedalus and Ariadne. Those three had come together on the little platform from which they had launched arrow and boomerang and shot. They spoke together furtively in the secret language, and at last Minos called something to the herald.

The horns keened a last fanfare, and the herald shouted hoarsely:

"Let Gothung the Northman come now to the palace of Knossos. Let him bathe, and rest from the ardor of the trials he has passed. At sunset, let him come to the sacred hall of the double ax.

"There he will receive all that the favor of the Dark One has bestowed upon him. The robe of Minos will be placed

74

upon his shoulders, and he will take his place among the gods. Cybele will be wed to him. And he will take up the double ax of war and peace that is the sign of the Dark One's regency."

Theseus touched the hot, smooth brass thigh of Talos.

"Tell them," he whispered, "that I shall do that."

The great voice boomed out obediently.

"Now," breathed Theseus, "lead the way to Knossos! I shall follow you."

Talos stalked back toward the massive gate, and Theseus staggered after him. It took all his strength to walk. Yet he contrived to stride boldly, to hold his yellow head high. Even if he should die now, he thought, from some warlock's trick, or a cowardly blade in his back, it would be in the midst of a triumph that must at least have shaken the power of Minos.

As he moved, a hushed and voiceless sound ran among the still-seated thousands. It seemed to hold a breathless surprise. There was relief in it, and dread. And also, Theseus thought, disappointment.

The great portal was opened for them at the end of the arena. Theseus paused for a moment in it, looked back. The crowd was beginning to rise, with an increasing murmur of awed and excited voices. Minos and Daedalus and Ariadne had gone.

Theseus followed the long strides of the brass man through the streets of Ekoros, toward the mighty pile of Knossos. This was a rich suburb, far different from the squalid quarter where he had met the palanquin of Ariadne.

The stone-paved streets were wider, clean-swept. There were no open sewers, no naked babies playing. High stone walls shut the villas away from the road, and only the trees of secluded gardens looked above them.

Evidently a rumor of the outcome of the games had already passed through the town. For the street was clear. The only people Theseus saw were lying on their faces in the intersecting alleys. A hushed silence followed him. Only once, from a huddle of rags, a woman's thin voice quivered out:

"Oh, new Minos! Pity your people, in their want. Clothe them, in their nakedness. Feed them, in their starvation. Remember that you were human once, and spare them from the terror of your power!"

Even when they came to the long mass of the palace, upon

75

its low eminence, none appeared to greet them. Theseus heard only distant whispers and far, hurried steps, merely glimpsed fearful figures hastening down dark endless corridors.

For all his anxiety and fatigue, he felt an awe at the vastness and the splendor of Knossos. The intricacies of its courts and corridors and lightwells and stairs and piled-up rooms bewildered him. But everywhere were rich tapestries, matchless frescoes, jars of purple gypsum—marks of wealth that woke Captain Firebrand in him.

"What a place," he murmured, "for us to loot!"

The floor beams creaked rather ominously beneath the tread of Talos. But he guided Theseus through the hushed corridors, and across an immense, flagstone-paved central court, and down a wide stair toward the river.

His fatigue half forgotten, Theseus was staring with a breathless elation at all the rich splendor they passed. It was his! He had won it, in the games. And it was going to be formally bestowed on him, after sunset—unless some warlock's trick intervened!

But not his for long, he knew. For he had won it, not for himself, but for the people of Crete, and his own Attica, and all the world. His next task—if, indeed, he had won anything —was to crush the priests and warlocks, end the cruel worship of the Dark One, shatter the reign of wizardry.

Then—well, the long habit of wandering had grown too strong to be easily broken. There was Egypt, with ancient wonders of its own. There were the strange far lands of the East. And, doubtless, other stranger lands beyond them.

Talos stopped beside a doorway.

"These rooms are yours, master," he boomed softly. "The slaves within will bathe you, serve all your needs. Rest until the sun has set. I shall wait by the door."

And Talos abruptly became perfectly motionless, in an odd way he had, so that he looked precisely like a huge statue of polished brass. Simple cunning was set upon his huge bright face, and the flame-yellow eyes stared fixedly.

Theseus walked wearily past him, into a rich apartment, illuminated from a white-plastered lightshaft. The walls were bright with lively scenes from the arena, graceful youths and girls vaulting over savage bulls. The cool rooms were furnished in the richly simple Cretan fashion, with rugs and low couches.

Two slaves showed him into the bathroom, lifted him into

a long bronze tub. Dissolving the grime of dungeon and arena, the hot soapy water felt very good. He didn't even mind the sting of it in his shallow wounds. He was beginning to feel very sleepy.

For a few moments his attention was held by the novelties of running water, drains, and a toilet that flushed. But his eyes were half closed when the slaves lifted him out of the tub. They toweled him, rubbed fragrant oil over his wounds, carried him to a low couch. He was sound asleep before he touched it.

It was dusk when Theseus woke, and a slave was entering with a flaring clay lamp. He sat up on the couch. His body had stiffened, the wounds were throbbing and swollen, and he felt a ravenous hunger. But no food was offered him.

"Come, Northman," rolled the deep voice of Talos. "The gods are waiting for you, in the sacred hall."

Still naked, Theseus rose and followed the brass man again. Flaming wicks lit the way. Once more they traversed the maze of courts and corridors and stairs, bewildering with the afterthoughts and alterations and additions of a thousand years. Theseus glimpsed slaves, kneeling as they passed, and said to Talos:

"Tell them to follow me."

"That is forbidden," the brass man rumbled. "Only the royalty, nobles, warlocks, and rich may enter the hall of the double ax."

"It is forbidden no longer," Theseus said. "For I am claiming the throne for the people of Crete, and I want them to be present. Bid them follow—all the artisans and slaves."

Talos looked back, his bright simple face perplexed.

"Minos would not like that."

"But I am the new Minos," Theseus said, "and I command it."

Still doubtful, the great voice of Talos boomed out the call. Theseus was aware of hushed and apprehensive steps, following behind them.

At last they came into the solemn vastness of the sacred hall, whose huge square columns were graven with the double ax. Weirdly colored flames leaped above tripod braziers shaped like bulls' heads. A black-curtained altar was covered with a white cloth, and a polished ancient ax of black obsidian lay upon it. Black-robed priests knelt beside it. Before it, robed in white and black, stood Minos and Daedalus.

77

Talos halted before them, rumbled:

"Here is Gothung the Northman, who was today chosen by the Dark One to take the throne. He is ready."

Standing beside him—suddenly extremely conscious of his empty-handed nakedness—Theseus looked into the face of Minos. It smiled back at him, dimpling, and the small eyes, in the flickering light of the braziers, seemed to twinkle with an expansive merriment. Minos looked past Theseus, at the slaves and artisans filing silently into the hall. He chuckled, and his silken voice said:

"Scourge them out!"

But Theseus lifted a protesting arm.

"Stop! I called them to follow me. For they are the people of Crete, and they are going to be the new rulers. I claim the throne for them. I warn you now that the reign of the warlocks and the Dark One is ended!"

White-robe and black looked at one another. The gnarled dark face was inscrutable as the dimpled rosy one. It seemed to Theseus, however, that an unholy glee had flamed for a moment in the hollow black eyes of Daedalus. But Minos smiled again.

"Let them stay," he said softly, "and see their god!"

The kneeling priests began a low, solemn chant, in the secret tongue. The wizard Daedalus, his hollow voice choked and snarling, called:

"Come forward, Gothung the Northman. Receive the vestments of Minos, take your divine bride, accept the double ax of the Dark One, and assume your place among the gods."

Striving to conceal a shiver of apprehension, Theseus went forward to the altar. At a signal from Daedalus, he knelt before it. Chanting in the secret tongue, the warlock lifted the white robe from the shoulders of Minos, draped it over him. The priests were abruptly silent. Rising, Theseus felt a hush of expectancy, saw eyes seek a dark doorway beyond the altar.

He looked, and Ariadne entered. She carried a silver lamp, and its rays shone red in the glory of her hair, white on her proud face, green on her long, loose robe. The white dove was fluttering on her shoulder. She came around the altar, and walked with a regal grace toward Theseus.

Theseus watched her face. It was white, frozen. Her features were cold as some lovely marble statue's, her green eyes dark and frosty with a scornful hate. She paused before The-

78

seus, looking beyond him. The sepulchral voice of Daedalus croaked:

"Through Ariadne, who is her vessel, daughter of Minos and sorceress of the serpent, the All-Mother Cybele takes him who was Gothung the Northman to be her honored husband, and welcomes him into the circle of the gods."

Ariadne stood proud and straight before Theseus, and still her cold angry eyes refused to see him. The dark claws of Daedalus lifted away the loose robe. She was left in a sea-green gown, whose tight scanty bodice revealed all her womanly splendor.

The deep rusty voice of Daedalus rang hollowly: "Do you, Ariadne, the vessel of Cybele, take this new god to your heart?"

The white dove fluttered back to the shoulder of Ariadne, and the silver serpent writhed about her waist. Its eyes were crimson gems, Theseus saw, that glittered evilly. Her golden voice faint and cold, she said: "I take him."

Theseus stood still, and saw a pale flush come up into her white skin. He relaxed a little, and dared to grin at her helpless wrath. Things were proceeding unexpectedly well. But Daedalus croaked at Ariadne:

"Then greet the new god with a wifely kiss—for you are now his bride."

The face of Ariadne went whitely tense, and the green eyes flamed. Theseus grinned again.

"We have already quarreled over the duties of motherhood," he told Daedalus. "Let us now forgive her womanly temper. I shall find time presently to teach her the obligations of a wife."

The warlock's gnarled face twisted into a black mask of hate. His sunken smoldering eyes stared for a long time at Theseus, as if their sinister power would consume him. At last he turned, shaken as if with a stifled fury, to the stone ax on the altar.

"Being the hand of the Dark One," he croaked hoarsely, "I offer the new Minos the sacred ax, whose twin blades are the crafts of war and the arts of peace, that is the token of the Dark One's regency." He reached for the worn ancient haft, but:

"Stop!" hissed the silken voice of Minos. "He is not yet a god!"

There was something impish in the rosy, dimpled smile, and the merry little eyes sparkled with an unwonted glee. Pink and stout without his robe, Minos bounced to the side of his daughter, whispered softly.

Apprehensively watching, Theseus saw the frigid white features of Ariadne break into a dazzling smile. She looked back at him, and her green eyes flamed a merciless triumph. Eagerly, her golden voice pealed:

"Wait! I see my duty. The new god shall have the salutation that is due him!"

Eagerly, she came back to Theseus. The white dove fluttered for balance, and ruby eyes glittered from the twisting serpent-girdle. Smooth and white and warm, her arms slid around the tense shoulders of Theseus.

"My divine master!" Her voice was a golden taunt, suave mockery shone in her long green eyes. "A kiss!"

Theseus knew that Minos had trapped him. Desperately he sought escape. He caught the smooth shoulders of Ariadne, thrust her roughly back.

"You refused it," he said. "Now wait till I am ready."

But Minos smiled his pink baby-smile, and the blue eyes twinkled. And Theseus discovered abruptly that he was held fast by unseen bonds, as he had been in the arena.

"Now, my lord." The eyes of Ariadne sparkled. "One kiss!"

Her long white body pressed close to his again, and he could make no move. Deliberately, her hot red lips sought his own, clung. Theseus abruptly felt the slackening of her arms, the new looseness of the white robe of Minos. And Ariadne stepped back from him, with mimic astonishment on her white face.

"Who are you, redhead?" her whisper mocked him. "And where is the godly spouse of Cybele?"

Released from those fetters of wizardry, Theseus looked despairingly down at his hands. They were lean and tanned —his own, not the huge sunburned hams of the Northman. They clenched, impotently.

He heard the soft faint tinkle of the laughter of Minos.

"Here, Talos!" whispered the silken woman-voice. "Here is the prisoner you have sought—the pirate Firebrand! He has stolen my robe! Seize him! Throw him into the deepest dungeon, to await the justice of the Dark One."

With a triumphant snarling sound, Daedalus tore the white robe from Theseus, wrapped it back about the pink pudgy

shoulders of Minos. The ruler was trembling with soft laughter, and the small merry eyes were almost hidden in his rosy
smile.

"But we were placing my successor on the throne," he
sobbed through the laughter. "Where is the Northman?"

The floor creaked, as Talos strode toward Theseus. In the
instant that was left to him, Theseus seized Ariadne, crushed
her long body against him so hard she gasped with pain. "This
is not the end," he breathed, "my bride!"

Deep within him, however, he feared that it was. He re-
called the calm wager of Minos on Gothung. Suddenly he
was certain that the rosy, jovial little warlock had penetrated
his guise at the beginning, that his victory in the arena and
this delayed exposure had been but an idle gambit—a game
to break the tedium that thirty generations of life must become.

The hot resistless hand of Talos crushed down on the arm
of Theseus, dragged him away. Looking back, he saw that
Minos still quivered with laughter. Ariadne was staring after
him with a curious startled expression, her face white as the
fluttering dove.

THIRTEEN

THE DUNGEON, lost somewhere beneath the rambling maze of
Knossos, was not unlike that in which Theseus had awaited
the games. A square, granite-lined pit, sunk deep in living
rock, it was damp with dripping water, cold with a bone-
piercing chill, foul with old decay. Theseus was alone in it.

No faintest ray of light, however, reached the pit to mark
the passing days. No sound filtered to it from the life above.
Theseus knew there must be guards somewhere in the stone-
hewn passages above, but he heard no voice or step. The
dungeon was a tomb of living death.

Lying in that other pit, before the games, Theseus had
boasted that a man might escape from such a place—if he
had to. Now, Theseus saw, he had to. And he tried the plan
that he had made.

He had waited endlessly for the guards to come with food. But no food was brought. He seemed as completely isolated as if he had been the only man alive. The justice of the Dark One, apparently, began with solitary starvation.

Theseus felt sure that it must be someone's duty, however, to ascertain from time to time if he still survived. And, when every hope of finding escape by the strength of his own hands was gone, he began calling at intervals into the blackness above:

"Ten talents of silver for a message to Admiral Phaistro!"

Ten talents of silver was four times a man's weight of the most precious metal. One talent was vast wealth. Ten was enough to excite the cupidity of any man. But the voice of Theseus rang hollowly against the bare, hard stone, and died into silence, and there was no response.

He called the words again and again, until his voice was gone. He slept, woke, croaked his hoarse appeal, slept and woke again, and whispered it. Time was short, he knew, when his strength and sanity would last to carry out the plan.

"Naked one, what silver have you?"

At first he could not believe that he had heard that cautious, fearful whisper. He lay still, trembling and breathless on the harsh cold stone. It came again, faintly:

"Doomed one, where is your silver?"

It was real! Theseus tried to quiet his sick shuddering, sought voice and strength and cunning. Chilled with dread of some blunder that might destroy this last tiny hope, he gasped into the dark:

"I have two hundred talents of silver—besides three hundred of gold, and twice that weight of bronze and tin, and forty jars filled with cut stones and jewelry—that Captain Firebrand took from a hundred rich ships of Crete and Egypt and the northern cities. It is buried on an island, and guarded with a wizard's spell, and only the wizard and I can find it."

There was silence in the darkness. Theseus shivered to a fear that he had failed, that the guard had gone away. But at last the whisper came:

"All the silver in the world, pirate—and all the gold and bronze and tin—would not buy one day of freedom for you. For the guard who set you free would doom himself to the justice of the Dark One. And all the treasure in the world could not save a man from the warlocks and the gods."

"But I don't seek escape," whispered Theseus. "I wish

merely to bargain for a service. If I am going to the Labyrinth, I have no need of that treasure on the island. I am
willing to betray its hiding place, for a service."

"What," came the fearful whisper from above, "is that
service?"

"It is one that Admiral Phaistro alone can render." Theseus
brought bitterness into his voice. "I was betrayed by one of
my officers—a man who had been my best friend. He seized
command of my ship, and set me adrift on the helpless hulk
to be wrecked on the rocks of Crete. I wish to bargain for
revenge against the Dorian pirate, called Cyron the Gamecock. Only the admiral can give me that."

Black silence. A drop of water fell with a tinkling crash
into a cold foul pool. Again silence. A sob of breath from
above, and a muttered curse, as if avarice and fear battled in
the guard. Doubtfully, at last:

"How do I get mine?"

"You can trust Phaistro," urged Theseus. "If he comes
here, the secret will be worth ten talents."

"Or my life!" came the mutter. Silence again, and the
shattering ring of another water drop. "The admiral has need
of your hoard," came the yielding whisper. "I'll tell him to
come—if he dares!"

Theseus shuddered with hope, turned weak again.

"Wait!" he called. "Tell Phaistro also that it is useless for
him to come, unless he can find and bring with him a certain
Babylonian cobbler, who has lately arrived in Ekoros. The
cobbler is a squat little yellow-brown man, with the features
of a frog. His name is Snish."

"But what," hoarsely whispered the unseen guard, "is the
need of a cobbler?"

"The cobbler is also a wizard," breathed Theseus, "and my
friend. He aided me to bury the hoard, and guarded it with
his arts. Neither of us can find it, or give directions for the
finding of it, alone. For each possesses only half the secret.
That is the spell."

"I shall tell the admiral," promised the guard. "But, pirate,
if this is all a lie——" The threat died in his throat, and he
muttered: "What further injury can be done a man already
awaiting the justice of the Dark One?"

There was silence. The drops of water crashed, loud as the
fall of crystal towers. The shattering falls were far apart. The

nerves of Theseus grew taut as he waited for each, and his body jerked to the shock, and again he waited through another tense eternity.

A cold shadow of apprehension lay across his spinning, weary brain. For there was, in fact, no such buried hoard. All the loot of the pirate crew, in the time he had been with them, had not amounted to half of what he had enumerated. But a tithe of that had fallen to the share of Captain Firebrand. And he had spent it with a free hand in the markets and the wine shops of a dozen cities, had flung it, more freely yet, to people in want from the wars and the taxations of Minos.

"All Cretans are liars." That was a proverb spoken from Thebes to Troy. A race of liars might well become adept at detecting falsehood. But this invention was now his sole hope of life, and the reeling brain of Theseus clung to it grimly.

Once he dropped into sleep. He dreamed that he had safely mounted the throne of Minos, that lovely Ariadne was his own. But she fled from him, into the Labyrinth of the Dark One. He followed, and found her amid the horrors of that dark, cavernous space, and kissed her. And she changed in his arms to Snish.

The crash of a water drop awoke him, a nerve-shattering avalanche of toppling crystal peaks. He lay on the wet, foul stone, and waited in an agony of tension. The drops crashed and crashed again, measuring intolerable ages.

Theseus thought that he was dreaming again, when he heard the scrape of a foot above. But there were cautious whispers and the muffled clatter of a sword striking stone. Lowered fearfully, he heard the precise, familiar voice of Admiral Phaistro:

"Captain Firebrand?"

"Yes!" Theseus gasped for breath. "Admiral—"

"Silence!" The voice was stifled, frightened. "We'll come down to you."

Still there was no gleam of light. A lock clicked faintly. Men whispered, breathed heavily with effort. There was a heavy creaking, a muffled brazen clang, a choked curse. He knew that the barred trapdoor had been lifted.

Something splashed in a foul puddle beside him. He found the end of a rope ladder, steadied it, as someone descended. He gripped an arm in the darkness, whispered:

"Who is it?"

The reply was no more than a muffled buzz, but he recognized the nasal tones of Snish. The little wizard's body was shuddering and clammy. His breath wheezed through tight wrappings about his head.

"Silence!" The voice of the admiral was thin and dry with fear. "And we dare make no light, for the ears and the eyes of the warlocks are keen!'

He dropped from the ladder beside them, found Theseus with quivering hands.

"There's no time to waste," he gasped. "My marines found this cobbler in a shop. He says he is no wizard, and he was using another name than Snish. But he is a Babylonian. I shall remove his gag."

"He is the wizard," said Theseus. "But let the gag stay. He can use his spell without words—if he wants to avoid being tortured for knowledge of the treasure on the island, and then, perhaps, flung to the Dark One."

Snish trembled more violently and emitted protesting nasal sounds.

"Hush!" The admiral's voice was a startled croak. "Don't speak of—that one. Not here! For we are close above the Labyrinth."

His thin fingers sank frantically into the arm of Theseus.

"And hasten!" he begged hoarsely. "Coming here, I risk my name, my position, my life. I myself am in danger of—that one. So speak quickly. Tell me where I can find your buried hoard. And where the fleet can trap this bearded Dorian—for the Gamecock has slipped through my hands again and captured another trader."

"Then come." Theseus led the admiral away from Snish, toward the corner of the foul cell. "The wizard need not know my part of the secret. And his spell requires no words."

"Hurry!" Phaistro was trembling. "The odor of this place would sicken a rat! And the danger—"

Theseus heard the sudden change in the admiral's voice to tones eerily familiar. The admiral was abruptly taller than himself. The words became a startled gasp, and there was a sound of tearing cloth. Theseus thrust himself free of the frantic clutching hands, slipped back toward the ladder.

"Help!" he shouted. "A trick—a trap! The prisoner has attacked me, stripped me!"

His sobbing voice was the voice of Admiral Phaistro. He

caught the ladder, that was already swaying to the mad climbing of Snish, swarmed up it at the little wizard's heels.

"Fools!" bellowed the admiral. "Stop him! He's trying to escape!"

But the admiral spoke in the voice of Captain Firebrand. He splashed frantically about the pools in the yet-unfamiliar cell, groping frantically for the ladder. Theseus reached the door, and quick, tense hands pulled him through.

"Master, are you hurt?"

"No, praise to Minos," rapped the precise new voice of Theseus. "But the pirate's treasure is all a lie—one worthy of a good Cretan. He assaulted me—planning, no doubt, to murder me under the darkness and escape in my clothing."

Unseen men were straining frantically. The massive bronze grate fell again, with a dull, heavy sound, muffling the screams and curses from below. Locks snapped. A slave wrapped Theseus in the loose robe that the admiral had laid aside before he descended the ladder.

"Quick!" whispered Theseus. "We must escape before his uproar calls other guards! Or we'll all face—that one! Firebrand's hoard was a lie—but still I'll see that you are all rewarded. Let's get out of here!"

Frightened guards led the hurried, furtive way through confused black passages, up long ramps, through a series of locked doors, and at last into one of the deeper palace magazines, where rows of huge jars held oil and wine. Finally a side door let them into an alley beneath the starlit bulk of Knossos, where a palanquin was waiting.

Theseus relaxed, trembling, on its scented cushions.

"Back home," he said anxiously, "before we are discovered!"

"But there's no danger now," said the servant, who had helped him into the litter, in the tone of one who enjoys his master's confidence. "We have been aboard often enough by night. Men will merely laugh and whisper that the admiral is wooing his goddess again."

The servant made a hollow chuckle.

"It's unfortunate that the pirate lied, but at least the trickery was not all his own. If he knew that you had captured his old comrades two moons ago, sold his men to Amur the Hittite, and already sent the Gamecock ahead of him into the Dark One's Labyrinth!"

The servant laughed thickly in the darkness.

Fourteen

THESEUS LAY between scented sheets of fine Egyptian linen. He opened his eyes on a long room. The frescoed walls showed graceful girls in a harvest dance. Hinged window screens of tinted oiled parchment were open, to reveal a quiet garden where birds sang in pomegranate trees.

The surroundings were all of rich luxury and high-walled security, but Theseus could not help a cold shudder of fear. He rubbed the smoothness of the sheets, and buried his face again in the fragrant pillow, afraid that he would yet wake up in the foul darkness of the pit.

For the success of his desperate plan seemed still a dream. He could hardly credit, even now, the splendor of this hilltop villa, to which the frightened slaves had brought him. The midnight feast that the chamberlain had set still seemed a vision of his starvation-goaded brain—and he was ravenous again.

But he remembered the chamberlain's laugh about his old companions' capture, the Gamecock already sent to the justice of the Dark One. That stiffened his dream into hard reality, sobered his incredulous joy. He was awake, all right, and he had things to do—Cyron had to be avenged!

He sat up on the bed. A tin mirror propped on a marble table showed him the sharp, narrow face of Admiral Phaistro. He made a grimace at the bulging forehead, womanish red lips, and retreating chin It was not a face he liked—but still he was mutely thankful for the gift of Snish.

"Did you call, master?"

The chamberlain, who hid the confidences of Phaistro under a countenance of rigid disapproval, was bowing in the doorway.

"Bring my breakfast," Theseus ordered.

"A quail's egg?" asked the servant. "And barley water?"

"Porridge with milk," amended Theseus. "A broiled fowl, honey cakes, and fruit—" Astonishment broke through the chamberlain's rigid face, and he cut short the order. "And send me the cobbler," he said. "The man is versed in certain small Babylonian spells, and he has promised to brew a wonderful philter for me."

"The master requires a wonderful philter indeed," returned the stiff-faced servant, "if he still aspires to the goddess. Your pardon, your breakfast! I rejoice that the master feels so hearty."

The bowl of porridge arrived—incongruously upon a long silver tray carried by two slaves. Snish came waddling behind them. Apprehension sat upon his seamed, wide-mouthed face, and his yellow popeyes darted about uneasily. Theseus sent away the slaves, and invited the little wizard to share his breakfast.

Snish, however, was in no mood to eat.

"Master!" he croaked, when his blinking yellow eyes had followed the slaves out of sight. "Do you know the peril that your mad plot has brought upon us?"

"I can see a danger," admitted Theseus. "If one man can get out of that pit, another can. And the presence of two admirals would make for confusion. Therefore, we must work swiftly. Try these Egyptian dates."

Bending fearfully, Snish shook his brown, bald head.

"It's worse than that, master!" he whispered. "Once your guise was broken—you must know that any close touch will turn you back to Captain Firebrand. And send us both to the Labyrinth! If these Cretan warlocks take us, my poor power will not serve again."

The whisper sank to a sobbing whine.

"Why, master, did you have to set Phaistro's marines after me?" He quivered, and tears sprang into the bulging eyes. "I had sold Tai Leng's jewels, and bought a tiny shop on a good street, with last and hammer and needle. Business is better here than in Babylon, and I had learned to be contented."

Snish blew his nose on a loose corner of his loincloth. "I was happy, master," he sighed. "I was busy all day—until the admiral's men came in the darkness, and broke down the shutters of my shop, and choked me with gags, and dragged me away without one word of explanation to the dungeons under Knossos."

The yellow eyes blinked. "Remember, master, I am no bold soldier of fortune. I am merely a luckless cobbler, with no stomach for such adventures as this. And had I not repaid my debt to you, master, on the day the games were played?"

"Try one of these honey cakes," said Theseus. "So you did aid me? I had wondered. You profess to be only a minor wizard, and yet you tell me that you defeated the warlocks of Crete?"

Snish shook his head, fearfully.

"I am the very smallest wizard, master," he protested anxiously. "My small powers are almost beneath the notice of the jealous warlocks of Knossos. Else they would have discovered and destroyed me long ago—as they will surely do yet, if you force me to defy them any further!" Paling, he shivered.

"The arrow and the boomerang and the wizard's shot went by me," said Theseus. "How?"

The yellow frog face faintly grinned.

"It was through the same small art that you already know, master," wheezed Snish. "After each god had launched his weapon, I changed you—too briefly for the eye to see the change—into the likeness of myself."

"Yourself?" muttered Theseus.

"The missiles were all," Snish told him, "aimed at your head. But Gothung was a tall man, and I am short. Therefore, the gods shot high. But I trembled lest they discover the trick!"

Theseus stared for a moment at the seamed yellow face, and tried to curtain the doubt in his eyes. He had felt that an effort of his own, a reckless defiance of wizardry, had helped deflect those shots. But the tearful face of Snish was earnest.

"These pickled olives are superb," he said. "Try them. The trick was very clever, Snish, and I thank you for my life. If Ariadne hadn't kissed me—"

"But she did!" whispered Snish. "And here you have flung yourself back into the same danger—dragging me after you!" The whisper sank. "Tell me, master—what are your plans? Since you are now the admiral, shall we not take the swiftest ship in the harbor and sail while we can?"

"No," said Theseus, and the thin features of the admiral turned hard with resolve. "I came here to crush the wizardry of Knossos—to end the reign of Minos and the dominion of the Dark One. And I shall!"

"Caution, master!" urged the fearful voice of Snish. "And don't shout! The warlocks have very keen ears for any such talk as that. Haven't you suffered enough from the folly of your purpose?"

"But don't you see?" protested Theseus. "The goal is already half won. As admiral, I am master of the wooden wall of Knossos. I can walk safely by Talos, the brass wall. There remains only the third—the wall of wizardry. That is all that stands before us, now."

"You are still Captain Firebrand!" Teeth chattering, Snish clung to the tall carved bedpost. "The warlocks had better look to their weapons—as doubtless they will!" He tried faintly to grin. "But perhaps Ariadne could tell you something about this wall of wizardry."

"Doubtless," said Theseus, wistfully. "If a man might speak alone with Cybele."

Snish grinned more broadly.

"Evidently, you are not familiar with the gossip in the servants' quarters." Anxiously, the little wizard caught the arm of Theseus. "Master," he begged, "beware of her kiss! Or we'll both end in the Labyrinth."

Theseus picked up the jeweled tin mirror and surveyed the thin, aristocratic face of Admiral Phaistro without enthusiasm.

"Women," he commented, "are very strange creatures. And goddesses, apparently, as well. When am I going to see her?"

"You are expecting a message today," Snish told him.

"What else have you learned in the servants' quarters?"

"Your financial affairs," Snish informed him, "are in a very bad way. You gamble recklessly, and spend tremendous sums for feasts and bribes, to maintain your position. You are deeply in debt to Amur the Hittite. That is why you were so anxious to secure the hidden hoard of Captain Firebrand. Amur, by the way, is coming to call on you this morning."

"The scorpion," muttered Theseus. "Thank you, Snish." He smiled. "Keep your ears open and your small arts ready to serve me—and perhaps you will live to be an honest cobbler yet."

Waiting to receive Amur in the great dusky hall, Theseus could not check a little shiver of apprehension. The Hittite, with his golden power, was almost as obnoxious as the warlocks. Hawk-nosed and sallow, lean-limbed and big-bellied, Amur left his palanquin in the court and bowed as he entered the hall.

"Your most humble slave, lord admiral."

For all his fawning smirk, however, his voice held a veiled

arrogance. Too small, too close together, his black eyes glittered, watchful and ruthless.

"Your slave beseeches upon you the favor of the gods." The husky voice had an almost oily softness. "And he regrets that his own dire poverty forces him to mention a certain small matter—that your notes are due again today, for five hundred talents of silver. Will it please the lord admiral to repay his slave that insignificant debt?"

Theseus met those snakelike eyes.

"The money isn't ready today," he said. "You will have to wait. As you know, the expenses of my position are heavy."

"Well I know it!" Amur abandoned the mask of servility, and his voice became a venomous hiss. "I've paid them for the last ten years." He shook a lean, yellow fist. "But I'm through paying them, Phaistro. Unless those notes are paid, Minos will have a new admiral—and the Dark One a new guest!"

"Wait." Theseus gestured protestingly. "You'll get the money." He tried to think. "I have learned where the pirate Firebrand hid his loot. A squadron of the fleet sails tomorrow to recover it. There will be enough—"

Amur's yellow claw made a fist again.

"You won't put me off with that." His glittering eyes, Theseus thought, were like a hungry rat's. "I have already learned how you spent the five talents you borrowed—to bribe the dungeon guards—and how the pirate duped you with his lies. If one word of your folly reaches Minos, it will take no more to break you, Phaistro!"

"I was a fool, last night," yielded Theseus. "But there are other ways of getting money."

"You always were a fool, Phaistro," snarled the Hittite. "But you have one way to obtain the money—and, unless you do, Minos will learn all he needs to know."

"One way?" repeated Theseus.

"So the goddess still frowns?" The Hittite laughed. "I warned you that it wouldn't be easy, Phaistro—not even for a lover of your famed skill—to unlock the treasury of Cybele."

"Well—" said Theseus, uncertainly.

"I'll give you one more night to try," Amur turned to go. "If she laughs at you again—well, the Dark One is always hungry." He put on the servile mask and bowed. "Farewell,

91

master. May the goddess favor you tonight with many kisses
—and the keys to her treasury!"

Alone, Theseus sat down on a couch and rubbed
reflectively at the weak chin of Admiral Phaistro. He lost any
regret for the ruse that had left the Cretan in the pit. A man
who made love for money— The chamberlain entered, carrying a tiny sealed scroll.

"Master, a message for you." His face was rigid. "It bears
the seal of Cybele."

Theseus broke the seal, unrolled the small square sheet of
papyrus. An eagerness checked his breath, as he read the
delicate Minoan script:

Mortal—if you indeed you feel yourself worth the
favors of a goddess—come to the old shrine in my olive
grove, after the evening star has set tonight.

With mingled impatience and trepidation, Theseus waited
for the fall of night. In the afternoon, officers came to see
him about certain naval matters. At first he attempted to put
them off, fearing to expose ignorance. But it soon appeared
that Phaistro concerned himself little with affairs of the fleet.
The officers wanted nothing more than the impression of his
official seal upon certain clay-tablet requisitions and reports.
The chamberlain brought the little graven cylinder, he rolled
it across the documents, the officers thanked him and departed.

When they were gone, the chamberlain reminded him that
he was due at the palace at sunset, to attend the reception of
a visiting Egyptian embassy. Theseus said that he was ill. The
chamberlain grimly promised him medicine, and objected that
his absence would please neither Minos nor the Pharaoh.

Theseus submitted to being bathed, oiled, and perfumed.
Slaves dressed his long black hair with scented pomades,
arranged it in buns and pigtails, attired him in an embroidered robe of purple silk.

And the chamberlain brought his medicine—a flagon of
strong brandy. Theseus drank enough to scent his breath, and
found an opportunity to pour a generous amount of the
remainder down a drain—wonderul, this modern plumbing! It
might be useful to seem drunk, but this was no night—of all
nights!—to be actually tipsy.

The palanquin carried him to the forbidding bulk of

Knossos. He shuddered, as if the very shadow of the ancient walls might break the spell of his guise. When he came into the frescoed splendor of the throne room—walking unsteadily, with the chamberlain holding his arm—he was appalled again to see the gnarled, hollow visage of Daedalus, the yellow, black-beaked mask of Amur, the rosy, dimpled smile of Minos.

The reception went on, however, and none of them seemed to consider it unusual that the chamberlain must hold the admiral's arm, whisper every necessary word into his ear.

The brown Egyptians entered, small, proud men. They spoke politely of the greatness of Minos, pompously of the grandeur of Pharaoh, fervidly of the friendship of the monarchs.

Theseus said only what the chamberlain whispered into his ear. As the affair continued, however, he permitted himself a few undiplomatic alcoholic slips of the tongue. He was beginning to enjoy the masquerade.

The evening star was low when he got back to the villa of the admiral. He left the chamberlain, waked the apprehensive Snish to come with him, and ordered the slaves to carry him to the old temple in the sacred grove of Cybele.

In the shadow of an olive, at the edge of the grove, he left the palanquin, telling the bearers to wait. Snish followed him toward the dim beehive shape of the ancient temple, protesting:

"Caution, master! Remember that one kiss will change you!"

Theseus chuckled.

"But we shall be in the dark," he said. "And you will be waiting here, when I return, to restore the likeness of the admiral!"

He walked boldly into the shadows, seeking Ariadne.

FIFTEEN

THE TEMPLE, erected over the fissure through which Cybele had been born from the mother earth, was a small, ancient beehive of unhewn stone. Rushes scattered the floor. Offerings of fruits and flowers lay withering upon a small altar, at the lip of the dank-smelling hole.

With a sharp hurt of disappointment, Theseus realized that the dark little chamber was empty. He waited, kneeling on the rushes as if praying before the earth womb. At last a rustle made him turn. His heart leaped with gladness when he knew that Ariadne had come.

For a moment, in the pointed arch of the entrance, she stood outlined against the night sky. She was tall and proud, and the light of the stars shone faintly on her hair.

"Mortal?" Her golden voice was muted. "You are here?"

"Goddess," whispered Theseus, "here I am!"

He rose from the altar and took her in his arms. She seemed at first cold and unresponsive, and even somewhat startled at his ardor, so that he began to wonder why she had made the assignation.

Presently, however, something in her seemed to take fire from his avid lips, and her mouth and her long, eager body returned his caresses. For a time neither of them felt any need of speech, and then:

"Well, goddess," whispered Theseus, "is any mortal worth your kisses?"

In a faint and shaken voice, she answered from his arms:

"There is one!" There was another time of silence, and then she added: "This is not what I came to find. For it was pity, not passion, that brought me here tonight. I came to bring warning that your enemies plan to destroy you, through your debts and your drunkenness and your indiscretions. I did not think to find—you!"

For a time again they required no words. Even Theseus, for a little space, forgot the purpose that had brought him to Crete. But presently a cold, slow movement of Ariadne's serpent girdle brought it back to him, and his arms tightened about her. "Would a goddess make jest of a mortal's love?"

The warm body seemed to quiver in his arms, and the golden voice was husky: "Never of yours."

"Then," pursued Theseus, "how would she prove her love?"

Ariadne kissed him, before she said: "I have been waiting for you to speak of that. For I know of your debt to Amur, and his threats. I came tonight to warn you to leave Crete while you could. But that was before—"

Her voice broke, and she clung to him. "In the treasury of Cybele," she whispered, "there are two thousand talents of silver. Tomorrow I shall send Amur a draft on the temple, for the amount of your debt."

"Thanks, goddess," whispered Theseus. "But I can't accept that."

Surprise stiffened her in his arms. They sat up on the rushes, and Theseus moved a little from her. Her warm hands clung to him. "Then, mortal," she breathed, "what do you desire?"

"If a goddess would prove her love of a mortal," he said softly, "she must offer more than silver. And there is another thing." His voice fell to a murmur. "A secret thing, called the wall of wizardry."

Ariadne made a little gasp, as of pain. Her fingers sank into the arm of Theseus with an abrupt, spasmodic force. For a long time she was tensely silent, trembling. Then she whispered faintly:

"Must you require the wall, mortal? For that is tenfold more precious than all the treasure in the temple. It is more precious than my life or my divinity. Must you take it?"

Elation leaped in the heart of Theseus. He had not known that Ariadne possessed the mysterious wall; he had hoped for no more than some hint of its nature. Striving to calm his hands and his voice:

"Love," he whispered, "that sets anything above itself is not love."

Her hot, fragrant arms crept around him. The cold, writhing coil of the serpent girdle touched his side. Her hair caressed him, its perfume half intoxicating. Her lips sought his.

"Kiss me," she whispered. "Forget your insane folly!"

But Theseus turned his face away from hers. "Then it isn't love," he whispered bitterly. "It is merely a jest." He pulled out of her arms and rose. "Farewell, goddess."

"Wait!" She rose after him, caught his arm. "You forget your enemies. I came to warn you—leave me, now, and you shall die before the dawn!"

Theseus pushed away her clinging hands.

"You don't understand the love of mortals, goddess, if you think that threats will buy it." He caught her tall, quivering body, drew her to him. "One kiss of farewell, because the love of mortals is real. Then I go—even, if must be, into the Dark One's lair!"

He held her to him, so close that he felt the thud of her heart. He kissed her soft throat, her seeking lips, her hair.

Then, firmly, he swung her from him, and strode toward the doorway of the little temple.

"Wait, mortal!" she sobbed after him. "Here—not to prove my love, but to save your life—here is the wall!"

Theseus came slowly back to her. In the faint starlight that filtered through the entrance, he saw that she was reaching into her silken bodice. She drew out some little object and solemnly pressed it into his hands.

Swiftly he fingered it. There was a thin, smooth chain that she had worn about her neck. Strung upon it, like a single long bead, was a tiny cylinder. It was warm from her flesh, the surface of it uneven with some graven design.

"This," he whispered, wondering, "is the wall?"

"It is," she told him. "It is a small thing, and simple—yet it holds a concentration af power greater than the Dark One's. Guard it well!"

"What is its power?" Theseus eagerly demanded.

Ariadne hesitated for an instant, and her tall body tensed again. "This is the secret of it," she breathed at last. "The man who holds it safe shall be master of Knossos, and no wizardry can prevail against him."

Theseus caught her shoulders. "Then you have given me Knossos?" She winced from his hard fingers. "Or is this another warlock's trick?"

"I have given you the wall—would you doubt me now?"

Theseus held her shuddering shoulders.

"If this thing *is* the wall," he demanded, "why do you carry it, and not Minos?"

"There was a reason why my father could not keep it with him," she whispered. "He trusted me—in all the years that I have lived, I have met no such mortal as you are." Her whisper sank. "Now, kiss me!"

Theseus clasped the chain about his neck and kissed her. When at last, breathless, they had drawn apart, Ariadne breathed:

"Now that I have proven my love, with the greatest gift that I could give, we must leave Knossos tonight—before my father's arts discover my betrayal. Have your fleetest ship made ready. My slaves will load it with silver. And we shall be sailing toward Egypt before the dawn."

Theseus touched the little hard cylinder on the chain. "But why must we take flight," he whispered, "when now the third wall is mine? Didn't you say that it would give me Knossos, and guard me against all wizardry? Then can't we claim the throne?"

Ariadne shook her head, against him.

"There is often an irony in the spells of wizardry," she whispered. "If the wall gave you Knossos, it might be for as brief a space as it was ruled by the Northman who was victor in the games."

She shivered in his arms. "Again, if the wall will guard you against wizardry, it will not defend you from an arrow or a blade or a strangler's cord. The wizards may recover it by cunning and force, and then you will be once more at their mercy."

Theseus lifted his head. "If the wall has any power," he said, "I shall use it."

Ariadne clung to him. "I have tried to warn you," she whispered. "Your enemies learned that you were coming here tonight. They have set a trap. You can't even walk out of this temple alive—without my aid. Yet you talk of unseating Minos!"

Theseus breathed, "And I shall!"

She laughed, half hysterical, and flung her arms tight about him.

"I know why you came to Crete," she cried softly. "But can't you see the mad folly of it? No mortal can hope to overwhelm the empire of my divine father—not even you, Captain Firebrand!"

Theseus stood for a moment, frozen. "So you know?"

"Did you think, Captain, that I could forget your first kiss so soon?"

"Still, knowing, you gave me the wall?"

"That is the reason." Her voice reflected scorn. "Would I give it to the drunken weakling, Phaistro?"

Theseus was hoarse with wonderment. "And you would sail to Egypt with a pirate?"

"Yes, anywhere—with Firebrand!" Her quivering hands tugged at him. "Shall we go?"

Theseus stared down into the darkness. His mind saw all the splendor of her proud body, the flame of her ruddy hair, the flashing spirit of her cool green eyes. Her arms made a caressing movement about him. At last, sighing, he said gravely:

"I wish that my business were less urgent in Crete. But I can't abandon it—not even for a goddess. When Minos has been unthroned, and the power of wizardry shattered, and the dominion of the Dark One ended—then, perhaps, I shall seek you."

Her voice was choked, barely audible: "You would destroy my father—all my world?"

"I must. Can you forgive me?"

"I . . . I don't know." She was sobbing; he held her in his arms. "I love you, Firebrand."

Then Theseus glimpsed the sky through the arch, and said: "The morning star is rising. I must go—if I can pass these enemies. And—if the third wall is what you told me—by tonight I shall be upon your father's throne!"

She rose with him from the rushes. "I'll go with you," she said. "Wherever you go. Because I have betrayed my trust, and I can't face my father's anger."

"No." Theseus put her gently from him. "The danger is too great, until I have won." He kissed her. "There is a better way." He grasped the silken bodice, ripped it. "If Minos finds that you have lost the wall, it was taken from you by trickery and force, and through no fault of yours!" He crushed her in a last embrace. "Now go—I'll give you time to leave the grove. Farewell!"

Waiting, after she had vanished through the arch, he unclasped the thin chain, tossed the tiny cylinder of the third wall upon his palm. If enemies were indeed waiting outside, it might be more secure, for the time, anywhere than on his person. Another apprehension shadowed him: if Minos found it unwise to carry the wall, it might be equally unwise for him.

After a moment he crossed the little altar, lowered himself into the chill, musty fissure beyond. If Cybele had indeed been born from it, he thought, she must have emerged prematurely. For the crack narrowed swiftly, until it wedged his feet and caught his exploring fingers.

He found a tiny recess, well hidden from the surface, and thrust the cylinder and chain deep into it. The talisman would not be discovered by accident, he knew, unless some worshiper profaned this most sacred spot in Crete.

And knowledge of the hiding place, he felt, might well be a more secure advantage than possession of the wall upon his person. Ariadne had kissed him tonight—but she must have been the daughter of Minos for nearly a thousand years.

He dragged himself out of the dank-smelling fissure, leaving a few bits of skin, and hurried out of the temple, through the starlight and shadow of the ancient silent grove, toward the tree where he had left Snish waiting.

"Here, wizard!" he called softly. "Restore the admiral's guise!"

But silence replied. A louder call brought no answer. Theseus searched beneath the tree, peered up into the branches, ran to the next. But Snish was gone. Panic clutched at the heart of Theseus. Without the little wizard's aid, all he had won was gone. He was trapped again, without disguise.

"Here he is!" A sharp voice ripped through the night. "Take him."

Theseus stood motionless, shuddering. For that was the thin, angry voice of the admiral himself. Phaistro had escaped from the dungeon and the likeness of the doomed pirate—and, of course, had soon discovered where to strike. Ariadne, Theseus guessed with a new sinking of his heart, had known of the escape and the danger; why hadn't her warning been more definite?

Dim shapes flitted through the shadows of the olives.

"The pirate!" cried Phaistro. "Take him alive, for the Dark One!"

Sixteen

Theseus had come weaponless to the tryst; even the admiral's bronze blade he had left in the palanquin. For an instant he half regretted that he had left the wall of wizardry, wondering if its power might now have served him. But he set himself empty-handed to the matter of escape.

"Greetings, admiral!" he shouted into the shadows. "But you may find you had done better to keep the shape of Captain Firebrand!"

He crouched as he shouted, sprinted down a dim avenue of

olives. The shrill voice of Phaistro screamed angry commands behind him, and scores of men burst out of shadow clumps.

Cast nets spun about Theseus. He leaped them, ducked them. But one tripped him, and he went down painfully. A panting marine was instantly upon him. He grasped the haft of a thrusting trident, twisted it, heaved, sent the Cretan reeling into the darkness.

Kicking out of the net, he ran again. Three marines stood up before him. He flung the trident like a spear. The middle man went down. Theseus leaped between whirling nets, and ran on down toward the river.

The uproar pursued, and torches flared against the pale glow of dawn. No more men appeared ahead, however, and he began to hope that he had evaded Phaistro's trap. Once across the river, he could doubtless find some temporary hiding place; he might make himself a disguise less fickle than those of Snish; there would be time to plan whatever new attack that possession of the wall of wizardry might make possible.

But, even as he went at a stumbling run down a narrow, dry ravine, doubts returned to check his feet. Had Ariadne betrayed her father—or him?

"No!" he sobbed. "That couldn't be!"

He remembered the vital pressure of her clinging body, the hot magic of her kisses. He believed she really loved him. But, if he had a purpose more important than love, so might she. A goddess would hardly betray her own pantheon. After all, she was doubtless about fifty times as old as she looked—and the vessel of Cybele, besides! A kiss couldn't mean so much to her!

He paused for breath in a clump of brush—and abruptly all hope of escape was shattered. For a deep, brazen bellow rolled above the shouts of the men behind. He saw a torch carried high as the trees. Its rays glinted on the gigantic metal body of Talos.

The brass man came lumbering down the ravine. The flame-yellow of his eyes was as bright, almost, as the torch. Rocks crashed, and the ground quivered under his tread. Theseus crouched lower in the brush. For an instant, breathless, he dared to hope that Talos would go by. But the crashing stopped abruptly, and the giant stood above him like a metal colossus.

"Captain Firebrand," boomed that mighty voice, "you are

100

taken again for the Dark One. Probably you think you are clever. But you shall not escape me—not with all your tricks and masks. For Talos is no fool!"

The ravine's bank, at that instant, gave way beneath the giant's weight. He sat down ignominiously in a cloud of dust. Theseus leaped to his feet, darted on toward the river.

But Talos, moving in spite of his bulk with a terrible swiftness, recovered his footing. With three crashing strides, he overtook Theseus, caught his arm in a great hand whose metal was almost searingly hot.

"No, Captain Firebrand," rumbled the giant. "This time you shall certainly meet the Dark One. Talos can promise you that. And you may find, after all, that you are the fool!"

That blistering, resistless hand held Theseus until the admiral and his men came up in the gray increasing light of dawn. Phaistro trembled with a fresh rage to discover his own embroidered robe upon Theseus—somewhat torn from the race down the ravine. His marines stripped Theseus.

"Never mind your nakedness, pirate dog!" He spat. "Men need no clothing in the Labyrinth."

Theseus was presently conducted back toward the town. Sharp stones and briers injured his bare feet—for Phaistro had recovered the beaded buskins. Marching in a hollow square about him, the marines kept prodding him with their tridents. Talos stalked watchfully behind.

Hopefully, Theseus wondered about the fate of Snish. He saw no evidence that the little wizard had fallen into the trap. Perhaps his ever-belittled arts had still served to save him. But there was scant likelihood, Theseus thought, that Snish would come voluntarily to his aid—or small chance, perhaps, that he could defeat the wizardry of Crete again, even if he tried.

The sun had risen by the time they came through groves and vineyards into view of the great ancient pile of Knossos. The admiral, carried in his palanquin before the marching marines, shouted back at Theseus:

"Look well at that sun, pirate—for you won't see it again. Men don't come back from the justice of the Dark One."

They passed the dark Etruscan guards standing rigid at the entrance, and came into the winding confusion of the corridors of the palace. Night fell upon them again, for the sun was not high enough to cast its rays into the shafts. Lamps still flared in dusky passages.

A group of black-robed Minoan priests met them, armed with long bronze-bladed lances. Their leader reported to Talos:

"Minos is ready to sit in judgment at once. The prisoner will have no chance to escape again. He is to be brought without delay to the hall of the Dark One."

The marines fell back, and the black priests formed another hollow square. Lances drove Theseus forward again, and Talos stalked behind.

They entered none of the courts or halls that Theseus had seen before. The priests took up torches from a niche beside the way, and lit them from a red-flaring lamp. Unfamiliar turnings took them into long descending passages. There were no light wells, and the air had the dank chill of perpetual darkness.

At last they came to a massive double door of bronze. It was ornamented with huge bulls' heads, of the same metal, and green with age-old damp. Talos strode ahead of the priests, and his metal fist thundered against it.

At last the door opened silently, and the lances urged Theseus into a long, narrow hall. Its walls were massive blocks of Egyptian basalt, illuminated only with the dull, vari-colored flicker of a tripod brazier.

Upon a low dais, beyond the brazier, were three black stone seats. Black-robed Daedalus, the hand and the voice of the Dark One, sat in the center. White-robed, rosy face dimpled merrily, Minos was on his right. On his left, in green, sat Ariadne—motionless.

In the brazier's uncertain light, Theseus stared at her. She sat proud and straight upon the basalt throne. The white perfection of her face was serenely composed. Her eyes shown cool and green against the flame, and she did not appear to see him.

The white dove sat motionless on her shoulder, and its bright black eye seemed to watch him. The serpent girdle gleamed against her waist, slowly writhing, and the eyes in its flat silver head were points of sinister crimson.

Theseus tensed himself against a shuddery chill along his spine. He tried to draw his eyes from the enigmatic vessel of Cybele. It was hard to believe this the same being whose kisses had been so fervid in the ancient shrine.

While half the black priests stood with ready lances, the rest knelt, chanted. The reverberation of a huge brazen gong

102

—deep as the bellow of some monstrous bull—set all the hall to quivering.

Theseus stood, stiffened and shivering, until at last the gong throbbed and shuddered into silence. The three stood up, upon the dais. Framed in fine white hair, the rosy face of Minos dimpled to a genial smile.

"We, the lesser gods, have heard the charges against this notorious criminal, the Achean pirate, called Firebrand." The woman-voice was soft; the small blue eyes twinkled merrily. "It is clear to us that the weight of his crimes demands the prompt judgment of the Dark One."

Fat pink hands fingered the silk of his robe, and he smiled jovially at the tall, naked body of Theseus.

"Therefore," he chuckled softly, "we remand the prisoner to the Labyrinth that is the dwelling of the Dark One, to face his eternal justice."

He turned, and his blue eyes twinkled into the dark, skeletal visage of Daedalus. "Do you, the hand and the voice of the Dark One, concur?"

The hollow, musty voice of the gnarled warlock grated: "I concur."

With his rosy baby-smile, Minos turned to Ariadne. "And you, vessel of Cybele, who is daughter of the Dark One?"

Breathless, Theseus watched her. The green eyes came slowly to him. Some tremor of her body made the white dove shift its balance. But her eyes remained remote and cold, and her golden voice said faintly:

"I concur."

The dancing eyes of Minos came back to Theseus and the tall bulk of Talos, waiting rigidly behind him.

"The gods concur." Laughter sparkled in his liquid voice. "Now let the door to the Labyrinth be opened, so that the prisoner may cross the threshold of the Dark One to face his judgment."

Talos moved startlingly, like a statue abruptly animated. But Ariadne, with an imperious little gesture of her bare white arm, froze him into inert bright metal again.

"Wait," she said. "I've a gift for the prisoner."

Minos and Daedalus turned swiftly upon her. The pink, cherubic features of Minos forgot their dimpled smile, and the seamed dark face of the high priest twisted into a mask of frightful wrath. Protesting whispers hissed.

From beside her on the black throne, Ariadne lifted a long roll of papyrus.

"This is a copy of the 'Book of the Dead,'" said her even golden tones, "that was brought by the Pharaoh's ambassadors. It is intended for the guidance of the soul beyond the gates of death." Her laugh was a tinkle of mockery, and the green eyes were cold. "I believe that Captain Firebrand will have use for it."

The merry eyes of Minos and the hollow, flaming ones of Daedalus peered at her doubtfully. Minos made a little, impatient bouncing motion on his black throne. The rusty voice of the warlock croaked:

"The prisoner has no need of it. It is the custom that men should meet the Dark One as they came from his daughter, naked, with empty hands. And even the soul required no guidance beyond the Dark One's dwelling, for it will be consumed."

But the pink, chubby body of Minos was shaken with abrupt merriment. "My daughter jests," he sobbed. "Remember, the prisoner is her enemy. Let him take the scroll of death—and go ahead to use it!"

The slim white arm of Ariadne extended the scroll's long cylinder. Theseus came forward silent, and took it, contriving not to betray its unexpected weight. He searched her white, lovely features for some hint of understanding. Her face remained a serene, proud mask.

"Go, pirate," she said. "The Labyrinth is open."

Already shivering to the abrupt penetrating chill that had invaded the black hall, Theseus slowly turned. He saw that Talos had stooped to grasp a huge bronze ring-bolt fastened to one of the great square basalt blocks that paved the floor, was lifting.

Gleaming bronze limbs and torso splendid with bunched swelling muscles, Talos heaved mightily. The huge stone came slowly up, before the dais. A dark, acrid fetor rose up from the black space beneath, and a stillness of awful dread fell upon the hall.

Theseus saw that the priests were blanched and shuddering. The visage of Daedalus was a dark, stony mask; Ariadne's face was white, frozen, and Minos had ceased to smile. Theseus himself felt a weak sickness of terror.

Something in that dank stench loosened his knees and poured cold fear dust down his spine. It was a hint of something more than cold and wet and endless dark and ancient rot, a reek of something—monstrous!

The straining body of Talos made muffled ringing sounds, like the thrum of muted strings, and at last the grinding stone came fully upright. The pallid priests silently leveled their lances, and the great, urgent hand of Talos reached out, hot with his effort.

Theseus glanced back at the three on the dais. He managed a mocking grin, and waved the papyrus scroll at them, casually. He turned, and spat deliberately into the dark pit beneath the lifted stone, and walked casually toward it.

Yet he was shivering. He pressed the scroll against his side, to stop the shaking of it. He came to the brink of the pit. In the faint reflected light, he saw stone steps, leading down.

He bent, placed his hands on the brink, and dropped upon the stair. Waving the scroll in farewell, under the flaming yellow eyes of Talos, he walked down into that sharp and ancient fetor.

That huge gong sobbed again behind him; the priests were chanting. The stone ground. There was a dull and mighty crash. And all light was cut off, as the many tons of the basalt door fell back into place.

SEVENTEEN

THESEUS STOOD motionless for a time upon those stone steps that he could no longer see. The air about him was a cold, stagnant fluid. It stung his nostrils with that reek of ancient putrescence, troubled him with that foul hint of something—living.

The mighty jar of the falling stone rang for a space in his ears, and then he felt the silence. He knew that the men and the lesser gods of Crete must be moving out of the black-walled hall. But not even the tread of Talos came to him through the portal and the floor.

The silence was solid, frightful.

Even in the utter dark, however, and despite that appalling, paralyzing stillness, he sought a ray of hope. For he had passed the three walls of Crete, and now he stood, still living, in the domain of the Dark One.

The Dark One, he knew—or fear of the Dark One—was the real ruler of Crete. If the hungry toil-drawn thousands obeyed the edicts of Minos, and starved their children to pay tithes and taxes, and offered them to perish in the games, it was through that fear.

Theseus stood unbowed within the entrance to the god's dwelling, and he was not empty-handed. He had felt the unexpected weight within the papyrus scroll, when Ariadne gave it to him. Now, when his eager fingers broke the seal and ripped it open, they found a thing they well knew—the polished hilt of the Falling Star!

The steel blade had been taken by the Etruscans who first captured him, by his own design, in the street of Ekoros. He had not expected to feel it in his hand again. He made a hissing stroke through the musty dark, and breathed his thanks to Ariadne.

Gripping the sword, he started down the slippery steps.

"Well, Falling Star," he whispered, "if we are fated to rot and rust here, at least we'll seek the Dark One first—and find out if bright steel will cut the stuff that Cretan gods are made of!"

His groping hands could span the rough-hewn passage, reach the arch above. The slope was sharply down, so that the steps were narrow. He went slowly, counting the steps and testing each carefully before he set his full weight upon it.

After sixty steps there was a small square landing and a turning in the passage; after sixty more, another. Upon the third landing his foot crushed something brittle, and his exploring fingers found two crumbling skeletons.

He thought that the more delicate bones must have been a woman's. The two sets were intermingled, as if their owners had perished in a final long embrace. Oddly, the man's skull and a few others of the larger bones were missing.

Theseus left the remains and went on down, wondering what might be upon the fourth landing. Again he counted fifty-eight steps. But, where the fifty-ninth had been, there was—nothing.

Almost, moving with too great confidence, he had lost his

balance. He recovered himself, and climbed one step back. He could feel a faint current of fetid air, rising beyond that invisible brink. Faintly, his ears caught a whisper of moving water, somewhere far below.

He tried to shout, to explore the space before him with the sound of his voice. His first effort brought only a rasping croak. Resolutely he put down the monstrous fear that this half-expected chasm had planted in him, and called out hoarsely:

"Greeting, Dark One!"

For a long time there was no echo at all, as if Theseus' voice had fallen against some muting curtain. At last, however, the reverberations of his shout came rolling back, amplified and distorted, from a thousand ragged distant ledges. He knew that there was a cavern before him, vast and deep.

Reaching out carefully, he explored the walls with his fingers as far as he could reach. Smooth stone extended in every direction. He could discover no possible way of climbing up or aside, and even the questing tip of his sword could reach no possible footing before him or below.

He knew, now, why the unknown man and woman had chosen to die upon the landing. He guessed, too, why part of their bones were gone—and that he had not been the first to follow them.

Their bones, he thought, might be useful to him also.

Climbing back to the landing, he gathered up the woman's skull and an armful of bones. He counted and tested the slime-covered steps again, and came back to the one above the last, and dropped the man's thigh bone over the brink.

It struck no ledge which he could dare to drop. For a long time no sound at all came back from the chasm. Then there was a faint and distant splash, that whispered eerily against the unseen walls.

Patiently, he dropped other bones at different points along the step, and then began tossing them in different directions. All of them fell for a long time, as the first had done, and splashed faintly, until he tossed the skull.

That struck something before him, and almost level with the step. It rolled, with a thin, hollow, bumping sound, and the bumping ceased, and finally there was another tiny splash.

Several other bones struck that uneven surface, and some of them remained there. Not even by extending the point of the sword as far as it would reach, could Theseus touch anything. But, at last, when his ears and the tossed bones had told him all they could, he crouched and swung his arms and leaped flatfootedly.

For an instant he thought that he was falling short, and he had a hideous sick awareness of the deep black abyss beneath. Then he came sprawling down upon an uneven point of rock, and slid, and at last caught himself upon its projections.

Creeping at first upon bruised hands and torn knees, Theseus explored the ledge to which he had leaped. It was a narrow spur of rock, he found, thrusting out toward the bottom of that black stair.

The way through the dwelling of the Dark One was clearly thick-set with peril. The most of those thrust into the Labyrinth, he thought, must perish in this chasm he has passed.

Was the justice of the Dark One merely—death?

Lying there on the jagged damp spur, waiting for breath and strength, Theseus tried to recall all his knowledge of the Dark One. The deity was sometimes represented, he knew, as a gigantic monstrous thing, half bull and half human. For a moment he shuddered with dread of some such fearful entity. But he gripped the Falling Star.

"We have killed bulls," he whispered to the blade, "and men! Why not the Dark One?"

He rose to bare bleeding feet and started climbing the spur, tapping with the point of the sword like a blind man with a cane. Sharp edges cut his feet again, and his naked body shivered and grew numb with cold.

The spur brought him to a sheer ragged wall. There was no ledge that he could follow to either side, and he thought that this path had led to nowhere but death.

But he was alive, and hope would not die in him. Presently his exploring fingers found a slanted fissure, and he began to climb, carrying the Falling Star in his teeth. Progress was slow. His limbs were soon trembling with the strain of lifting his body by inadequate purchases. He felt that he was near the limit of exhaustion, when he came to a roof that jutted out above his head.

There was no passage upward.

He knew that he had no strength to climb back to the spur —nor was there much reason to return. Presently, he thought, his aching fingers and toes would relax and slip.

There would be another splash, unheard, from that black water.

He clung to the rock, however, and a breath of stale unsunned air touched his face like a ghostly wing. He clambered aside, and the current became stronger. He reached the lip of a narrow passage, and pulled himself through it, and came to a flat place where he could rest.

For a long time he lay there, breathing wearily, rubbing at aching muscles. At last he tried to rise, and drove his head painfully against the tip of a sharp stalactite, and crept on hands and knees to explore this new cavern.

He followed a winding gallery of water-carved limestone, that presently became tall enough so that he could walk again, and tap his way with the sword. There were narrow fissures that he could just squirm through, abrupt drops that he clambered down or skirted, cold pools that he had to swim.

Stone and water had fashioned strange formations. One, that his lacerated hands explored, was shaped queerly like an immense bull's head. A projecting boulder formed the head itself, and two curving stalagmites were like horns. The rock mass beneath held an odd suggestion of a gigantic human body.

That strange natural symbol of the Dark One stood in a wide cavity in a long endless gallery. Theseus dislodged a limestone fragment. The rattle of it rolled ominously against an unseen vault, and came back queerly amplified, so that it sounded like the far-off bellow of a monstrous bull.

The cave was a natural temple. If indeed, Theseus thought, he was destined to meet the Dark One, it should have been here. He was shuddering to an uncontrollable sense of supernormal dread. But nothing tangible challenged him.

At last he found an exit, and went on.

For an endless time, Theseus wandered through unending passages. He squirmed through fissures that tore his skin. He leaped unseen crevasses. For a space he was hungry, and the hunger passed, leaving only a light-headed weakness. Once he slept, woke chilled and stiff. Thirst tortured him, and he drank from a bitter pool.

Always he went on.

Then his foot knocked a pebble over a ledge, and the sound rolled above him, swelled into an angry bellow. He felt an ominous familiarity in the contours of the slope beneath his feet. And his groping fingers found that rugged anthropomorphic stone that had the head and horns of a colossal bull.

With a cold sickness in his heart, and a tremor of unquenchable terror, he knew that all his wanderings had brought him around a futile circle, back to this dark temple that was older than the race of men.

Had the Dark One been his guide?

A strong heart and the Falling Star might prevail against wood and brass and even wizardry—but not against the nameless, formless, voiceless shadow of power that haunted this unceasing dark.

So Theseus was hopelessly thinking, when a fearful voice spoke to him. It reverberated against the unseen vault, swelled until it was as mighty as the bellow of some colossal bull, and yet articulated words:

"Welcome, mortal, to my eternal abode! I have waited long for you. For I am hungered from fasting, and I thirst for a man's blood."

Theseus stood lifeless. That supernal bellowing voice held an incredible familiarity. Something moved in the darkness, however, before he could grasp that impossible recognition. It rushed upon him.

In a blind instinctive effort at defense, the nerveless arm of Theseus flung up the Falling Star. It rang against something hard. Something smooth and round and pointed came thrusting past sword and arm, and stabbed into his side.

It was like a monstrous goring horn.

Eighteen

THAT TERRIBLE horn grazed his naked flesh and lunged again. But Theseus automatically fended the second thrust away from his body with the Falling Star. For the horn came in like a heavy pike, and the instinct of many battles taught him how to deal with it, even in the darkness.

The Dark One fought like a man. Even the little grunt of

effort, as the horn made its third ripping thrust, sounded queerly human—until the echo of the unseen dome amplified it into a far-off bellow.

Grim confidence returned to Theseus. A god that fought like a man could be slain like a man. He gripped the steel sword, let that smooth lunging point slide once more past his body, and thrust where a man must be to hold it.

But his foot, as he thrust, slipped into an unseen hole. He dropped forward on his face. His sword hand struck a sharp edge of rock, and the blade went clattering out of his fingers.

Pain from his ankle sickened him. He dragged himself back to his knees, groping desperately for the sword. He found only cold blades of stone. Cold dread stiffened him as he heard feet rush toward him, felt that lunging horn.

"Now, mortal Cretan!" That rolling, distorted bellow was still mockingly familiar. "Die to feed your god!"

Theseus dropped flat again, let the weapon pass above him.

"I'm no Cretan," he gasped. "And we Greeks have a different rule of hospitality—it is the guest who must be fed!" His voice became a whispered prayer. "Here, Falling Star!"

The echoes rolled into silence, and a startled hush filled the cavern, until:

"Greek?" breathed the other voice. "Falling Star?" The whisper was human, anxious, breathless. "You . . . you aren't— You can't be . . . Captain Firebrand?"

Abruptly, Theseus recognized that haunting familiarity. "Cyron!" he cried. "Gamecock—it's you!"

That long, heavy horn clattered on the rocks—and shattered, so that Theseus knew that it had been only a loose stalactite—and the Dorian pirate lifted him into a hairy embrace.

"It's good to find you, Captain," sobbed the Gamecock. "Even though you have cost me a meal!"

"Better to find you," returned Theseus. "For I thought— half thought—that you really were the Dark One!"

"So I planned for every man they send down here to believe," whispered Cyron. "That ruse is all that has kept me alive, through the years since that metal giant dropped me through the portal—how many years has it been, Captain, since my ship was taken?"

"No years," Theseus told him. "It's little more than two moons since I sailed our prize to meet the Cretan fleet with that little Babylonian wizard—remember him?"

"Two moons!" gasped the Gamecock. "No more than two moons? Captain Firebrand, I've been lost in this frightful darkness for half a lifetime, surely. The cold and wet of these slimy, stinking caves have made an old man of me. Else the horn of the Dark One would have gored you through with the first lunge!"

"And you have met no Dark One," whispered Theseus, "save yourself?"

"I was half dead with terror," Cyron said, "when that metal monster tossed me into the Labyrinth. All the warlocks had promised me that their god would be waiting to devour me. But in all the years—or the two moons, if it can be so brief a time—there has been no god here but myself. I have played the Dark One only because even here a man must eat."

Theseus had found the Falling Star. His fingers caressed the polished pattern of the inlay in the cold hilt, the smooth clinging edge of the blade. In a soft, breathless voice he said: "Then there is no Dark One?"

"Not here, Captain Firebrand," said Cyron. "Though I had been crawling and leaping and climbing through these haunted galleries for half a lifetime—so it seemed—before I guessed it."

His fingers were touching the arms and the shoulders and the face of Theseus, like those of one blind. "It is good to find you, Captain," he whispered.

"So there is no Dark One!" Theseus murmured softly.

"Some chance freak of water and stone must have made this half likeness of a bull-headed man," Cyron said. "And some ancient Cretan, lost in these caves, found it. He was already afraid, and his own frightened cry echoed into the bellow of an angry bull. So the Dark One was born! Or so at least, after this weary time, the truth seems to me."

Theseus gripped the Falling Star. "The Dark One is a lie!" A newborn power rang in his voice. "All the sway of Crete— all the dominion of wizardry—is built upon a lie! It is fear that sits upon the throne of Minos. Fear that is the blade of wizardry. And fear without cause!"

He stood up, clutching the sword. "This truth is the weapon I have sought, Gamecock. We shall carry it back to the world above. For it is the sword that can scatter all the minions of Minos. It is the torch that can fire the wizardry of Knossos!"

Cyron grunted cynically. "Minos would not encourage you to speak," he said. "Nor would his subjects dare believe your blasphemy." He sat down on the wet stone. "Anyhow, it is an idle question, because we can't get out."

"We can try," said Theseus. "Now we have a reason."

"For all this time I've had a reason," muttered Cyron. "And I've tried. There's no way out. None save the portal through which we entered—and only the brass giant can open that."

Theseus rubbed at the stubble on his chin. "There's another way," he said. "You've just proved it."

"I?" Hope struggled with Cyron's doubt. "How?"

"When you spoke of the birth of the Dark One. Before the Dark One was known, you said, some lost Cretan must have wandered unwittingly into this evil temple."

"Well?" said Cyron.

"He didn't wander through the passage by which we entered," Theseus told him, "because that is a hewn stair that must have been planned by architects and cut by the labor of many men. Their masters must have known of the cavern already. So there must be an older, natural entrance!"

The Dorian grunted hopelessly. "Perhaps there is—or was two thousand years ago. But we've no way of finding it. I have followed a hundred winding passages away from this place of the Dark One—and always, in the end, here I am again!"

His teeth chattered, and his voice sank hoarsely. "Sometimes, Captain Firebrand, I think there is a real evil power in this horned stone, that guides men here to die, for the cavern floor about it is spongy with rotting bones."

Cold, shuddering, his fingers gripped the arm of Theseus. "Perhaps there *is* a Dark One!" he muttered. "Perhaps the deity merely lets us deny him for a jest, until, after a thousand blind circles, he brings us back to lay our bones before him."

"Don't say that—for there is no Dark One!" But the voice of Theseus trembled uneasily. "Come—at least, we can search for a way."

"I'll wait for you here," muttered Cyron. "In a day or two —with the Dark One for a guide—you'll be back—and thinking you had almost escaped." He grunted. "Perhaps when you come—if the warlocks have fed their god again—I'll have meat for you."

Theseus was silent for a little time. "I think I know how to find the way," he whispered at last. "The Falling Star will guide us!"

"A sword!" muttered Cyron. "It can't speak!"

"It has guided me across the desert and across the sea," Theseus told him. "My father told me that the metal of it fell out of the northward sky. And still, when it is hung by a hair, its point seeks the North Star."

Cyron grunted doubtfully. "Perhaps you can tell the directions, as you used to at sea," he muttered, "but what good is that, when we don't know which way to go?"

"Perhaps," Theseus said slowly, "I do. Anyhow, the Dark One will not turn us back unawares."

Cyron rose reluctantly. "Then lead the way," he said gloomily. "It will be a long one, for men stumbling in the dark. And probably—in spite of your sword—it will end here before this evil figure."

Theseus had pulled a single long hair from his head. He tied it carefully around the steel blade, at the little nick where it balanced. He waited patiently for the swinging sword to come to rest, then touched it with his fingers.

"This is the way that we must go." He held the blade, for Cyron to feel its direction. "On beyond the horned rock."

The Dorian followed him. It was not easy to hold any direction, even approximately. They came to blind endings, had to turn back, swing the blade again, try another corridor.

They both were weak from hunger, shuddering and stiff and numb with cold. Raw feet left unseen blood upon the rocks. Sharp ledges cut their naked bodies.

Cyron wanted to turn back. "I was never the resolute man that you are, Firebrand," he muttered. "I like a good fight—but a good meal more. And, if I go back to the Dark One, Minos will send me one. You are too hard, Firebrand. You are hard, bright metal, like your blade—hard enough to fight the gods."

"And," Theseus whispered grimly, "to conquer them!"

"Then go on," Cyron told him. "I am turning back."

"Not now, Gamecock," said Theseus, and touched him

114

with the Falling Star's point. "You are coming with me—one way or another."

Cyron started, rose stiffly. "Then I'll come alive," he gasped apprehensively. "Put away the sword! I know you jest, Firebrand—hope you jest." His teeth chattered. "But you're a hard man and set on your purpose. I'll come with you!"

They climbed on, through endless dripping passages. They swam foul black pools and crawled on their faces through slimy crevices, explored blind pockets and retraced their way, and forever swung the sword again to keep the same direction.

Then the time came when Cyron fell and would not rise again. "I'm done, Captain Firebrand," he whispered feebly. "Slit my throat and drink my blood, and you can go on. But I am done. There may be a way—but only light could show it to us."

"Then," Theseus said, "we shall have light."

Wrapped about his neck, where it was dry from his body heat, he had carried the papyrus scroll in which Ariadne had concealed the Falling Star. Tucked in it was a hard flint pebble, that he had brought from the cave of that monstrous stone.

He shredded a corner of the scroll, struck sparks from the flint with the Falling Star's hilt. The papyrus smoldered, burst into flame—the first gleam that Theseus had seen in all the Labyrinth.

"Light!" sobbed Cyron. "A light!"

"The book of the dead," said Theseus. "But it can guide the living."

They went on. Theseus extinguished the tiny torch, when it had shown them a possible path. A dozen times he lit it, and put it out—and always watched the smoke. At last there was a feeble drift aside. They followed it. And when the little flame went out again, the dark was not complete. There was a gray, lingering gleam.

Day!

Breathless and trembling, they climbed toward it. But a great boulder, sometime in the ages, had slipped to block the passage. The narrow open fissure would not admit their bodies.

Weak with exhaustion and want, ill with despair, they lay down under that tiny precious light. Slowly it faded above them, and there was only darkness. It seemed to Theseus, drifting into dull oblivion, that this must be the last night.

But he woke, presently, filled with a new hope and strength. A pale ghostly light was filtering again through the fissure, and it guided the point of the Falling Star. Weathered stone chipped and crumbled, and presently Theseus shook the inert limp form of Cyron. "Come on," he whispered. "The way is open."

His words roused the sleeping Dorian, magically. They squeezed through the passage that Theseus had cut, and climbed ragged lips of stone, and came out into a tiny beehive building.

Precious white moonlight poured through the pointed entrance arch. It washed the rush-covered floor, and flooded a tiny altar, where lay offerings of dates and barley cakes, a piece of smoked fish, a bowl of pickled olives, and a jar of sour wine.

"Where—" gasped Cyron. "What—" He fell before the altar, snatched the fish.

"This is the shrine of Cybele," Theseus told him. "The Cretans believe that their goddess was born of the earth and the Dark One, through the way we have come, to be the mother—" His mouth was full of dates, and he spoke no more.

The full moon stood high in the heavens, when at last they reeled drunkenly through the pointed arch. The olives of the sacred grove made black shadow masses under its silver flood. The Kairatos Valley lay dark and broad beneath it, and the sleeping city of Ekoros sprawled brown about the sinister hill of slumbering Knossos.

"We have come alive from the Labyrinth." The voice of Theseus was hushed and savage, and his hand quivered on the Falling Star. "And we have brought back the secret that will conquer Crete!"

Swaying with the wine, Cyron spat date seeds and grunted cynically. "But we have no token of proof," he muttered. "And blasphemy is the blackest crime. They would send us straight back to the Dark One—and make certain that we stayed!"

NINETEEN

THESEUS CLIMBED a little way back into the passage. He fumbled in a cavity, and found the thing he had left there—the tiny graven cylinder of the wall of wizardry, strung upon its silver chain. He fastened it about his neck.

Cyron, meantime, had wrapped the remainder of the food up in the altar cloth. They left the shrine, and dawn found them in an abandoned, brush-grown vineyard on the summit of a little rocky hill.

There they spread out their loot, and split the linen cloth to wrap their loins. The cool open air was incredibly fragrant and good, after the fetor of the caverns, and the rising sun was thankful to their long-chilled bodies.

They lay in the sun all morning, one eating and watching while the other slept. In the afternoon they found the thin shade of a gnarled abandoned apple tree, and Theseus talked of his plans, countering the muttered objections of Cyron.

"The Cretans won't believe us," Cyron maintained, "for every man who does thereby condemns himself to the Labyrinth."

"Perhaps," said Theseus, "but there are men who will believe—our pirates! They are slaves, now—those who are left alive—in the compounds of Amur the Hittite—so I learned when I was admiral. They'll believe."

Cyron wriggled his hairy brown body under leaf-filtered sun. "They might," he muttered. "But what if they do? They are a mere handful, starved and tortured and laden with chains, already beaten by the power of Crete."

"Then they have reason enough to rise," said Theseus. "As all the Cretans have! And the truth we bring will cut their fetters and be their swords. *There is no Dark One*—those very words will conquer Minos!"

"They are good ringing words," admitted Cyron, "but what are any words, against Phaistro's galleys and marines, and the Etruscan mercenaries, and the brass might of Talos, and all the power of the Cretan gods?"

Theseus fingered the hilt of the Falling Star. "The Dark One was the greatest god of Knossos," he said, "and we have conquered him." A faint smile of eagerness touched his drawn, stubbled face. "The vessel of Cybele has yielded." His face turned hard again. "There are only Minos and the warlock Daedalus and the Man of Brass—and, like the Dark One, they shall die!"

They left the vineyard when the sun had set, and walked down a road toward Ekoros. Theseus accosted a sweat-stained laborer returning homeward with his hoe, and asked directions toward the slave compounds of Amur the Hittite.

"That's a strange question!" The farmer looked at them curiously. "Most men are more anxious to leave the pens than to find them. But, if tithes and taxes force you to sell yourselves to Amur, take the left turn beyond the olive grove and cross the second hill—and watch that his guards don't kidnap you and drink up your price!"

Dusk thickened to night, and the full moon came up beyond the purple eastward hills, before they came to the slave compound. A tall palisade inclosed it, and guards leaned on lances at the entrance gate.

Dropping to all fours, Theseus and Cyron crept silently up through the weeds outside the barrier. Through the poles, they watched the chained slaves being driven in from the long day's toil.

All the fields about, the farmer had told them, the orchards, gardens, the vineyards, belonged to Amur. His were the brickyards, the pottery, the looms, the smelter. And all his slaves were penned here, like cattle, for the night.

The wind changed, and brought a sour, sickening odor.

In an open place, between the flimsy barrack sheds and the stone trough where the slaves were allowed to drink like horses, a fire burned low. In the bed of coals stood a huge pottery urn, taller than a man, soot-blackened. The urn rang, at intervals, with a dull and muffled scream of agony.

The Gamecock's lacerated hands were clenched.

"There's a man in the pot!" he whispered. "But what can we do?" His hairy body shivered in the weeds. "Two men, with one sword—against that wall and twoscore of guards! We'll be roasting, ourselves, in Amur's pot!"

"We have the Falling Star!" breathed Theseus. "We have at least one ally within—the one-eyed man, chained to yonder

118

post, is our Tirynthian cook, Vorkos. And we have a battle cry—*There is no Dark One!*" He gathered himself to rise. "Come on to the gate!"

But the pirate caught his arm. "Wait, Captain Firebrand!" he whispered hoarsely. "Here come fighting men!"

He pointed, and Theseus saw torches flaring on the road from Ekoros. Light glittered on the tips of lances. A silver horn snarled. Theseus and the Dorian dropped back in the weeds, to watch.

The torches came up to the compound's gate. A squad of Amur's yellow-belted guards led the way. Behind them four slaves carried the Hittite's yellow-curtained palanquin. Behind the palanquin marched a group of black Minoan priests, with lances.

Amur's voice rasped to the guards by the gate: "I have promised a gift to the gods. Three strong youths and three beautiful girls. They will be trained for the next bull vaulting, and any that survive will go to feed the Dark One. For the gods have favored me. My enemy, Phaistro, has gone to the Labyrinth for treason. And I am the admiral of Crete!"

His voice was a feral snarl. "Quick, officer! Light torches and drag out the strongest young men and the most beautiful girls—those that came in the last ship from the north—so that the priests of Minos can choose."

In the shadows, Theseus touched the arm of Cyron. "Wait," he whispered, "until the slaves are brought."

"I'll wait." The Dorian shuddered. "Even longer!"

Torches moved beyond the sharpened poles. Guards herded groups of slaves out of the barrack huts, made them stand in long lines. Still, at intervals, a hollow scream of agony came from the huge black urn.

Theseus heard the snarl of Amur: "The Northman still lives, after a day and a night in the pot? These pirates are tough sticks to break. But Gothung's fate will be a lesson to them to jump when the whip snaps."

Cyron tensed and shivered. "Gothung!" It was a muted, savage breath. "My steersman and my friend! Come, Captain Firebrand—we have waited long enough!"

"But silently," whispered Theseus. "Until we reach the gate."

With the hairy bearded Dorian stalking at his arm, Theseus came to the compound's entrance. The tall wooden gate had

119

not been closed since Amur's coming. Half a dozen guards stood about their watch fire, just within. It was a hundred paces to the central opening, where the urn sounded hollowly and the black priests were selecting their victims.

Well within the gate, where the light of the watch fire showed them plainly, Theseus paused and checked Cyron. He flourished the Falling Star, so that the fire shone red against its bright steel, and shouted:

"Halt! There is no need to send more boys and girls to die in the Dark One's game—none to send them into the Labyrinth to feed him. Because the Dark One is dead!"

A breathless, startled silence fell over the compound. Slaves and guards alike paused to stare, dumfounded. Theseus stalked forward, with Cyron at his side, so that the watch fire cut them in silhouette.

"I am Captain Firebrand!"

The sword was lifted again, and his voice peeled into the hush: "Here, with me, is Cyron the Gamecock. You all know that we both were flung into the Labyrinth, to face what your lying priests call the justice of the Dark One. Well, the Dark One met Athenian justice, instead."

The sword flashed crimson. "There is no Dark One—and never was! All the power and the wizardry of your masters is set upon a lie. Rise, slaves! Join us, fighting men!" His voice had a war horn's ring. "Comrade pirates, avenge Gothung! Down with Minos! Set men free from wizardry!"

That challenge broke Amur and the black priests out of their paralysis. Angry voices cracked. The eight priests, with lances leveled, came charging toward the gate. And Amur screamed a command for the guards there to seize the intruders.

The guards hung back, however, obviously impressed by the challenge of Theseus. Only their captain, after his men had failed to obey the command, rushed at Theseus with his long sword lifted. Steel met bronze, and the old delight of battle turned steel to lightning. The captain fell, and Theseus cried again:

"There is no Dark One!"

"That is blasphemy!" screamed the leader of the charging priests. "The Dark One will blast him down!"

But Theseus did not fall. He went on to meet the black priests. And Cyron, snatching the sword and shield of the fallen captain, followed him.

"Rise, comrades!" called the pirate. "Remember Gothung! There is no Dark One!"

Hoarsely, somewhere in the barrack sheds, that cry was repeated. It ran along the waiting lines of slaves. It echoed. It grew into a bellow of furious revolt. The slaves fell upon the guards, fighting with their very chains.

Theseus and Cyron met the black-clad lancers. Two against eight. But the first hewing sweep of the Falling Star cut the shaft of a lance, left a useless stick in the hands of the foremost priest. Cyron caught another on his shield, and his bronze blade ripped a throat. Then the guards came running behind them, echoing:

"There is no Dark One!"

That war cry rang through mad confusion. It pealed above screams and moans and hoarse commands and the furious clash of weapons. Not half the guards joined the revolt, nor half the slaves broke their chains, and for an endless time the issue hung in doubt.

Theseus battled in a mad world of fire and reeking blood and stinging sweat and smoke and darkness and weariness and screaming pain—and savage elation turned the Falling Star to a live and terrible thing in his red hands.

"Fire the barracks!" shrieked Amur, when the decision turned against his men. "Let them roast—to the glory of the Dark One!"

Amur's guards ran with torches among the flimsy, reed-thatched huts, in which half the slaves still were chained, and turned them to roaring pillars of yellow death. Red madness flickered back from Amur's close-set eyes, and he screamed from the yellow-curtained palanquin:

"Drive them all into the fire—the Dark One will find them there!"

But the mutineers had caught a new flame of strength and valor. Even the slaves in the burning huts broke their fetters, or pulled up the posts to which their chains were fast, and came out fighting.

The Falling Star cleft the skull of a black lancer. And Theseus discovered that the battle was done. The Minoan priests were dead, and all the guards who had not joined the mutiny.

Cyron gripped his quivering arm. "Catch your breath, Captain Firebrand!" gasped the red-dripping pirate. "You have earned it!"

Theseus wiped his blade and stared around him. The victorious survivors of the mutiny—in all, nearly two hundred men and women, slaves and former guards—were crowding away from the still-flaming ruins of the barracks, into the open area.

Screams of agony bubbled hollowly in the huge black jar.

"Gothung!" choked Theseus. "Still—living!"

He started toward the jar. But Vorkos, the one-eyed Tirynthian cook, was building up the fire about it. He pointed to a brown, shapeless being beside the coals.

"That's our comrade," he said. "It's Amur in the pot—and never I fanned my fire with a better will!"

Theseus walked among the survivors, greeting those who had been with him on the pirate galley. Then he mounted a pile of fagots, near where Amur screamed, and said:

"Men and women! You were slaves—but you have fought, and you are free. The thing that set you free is a truth that the Gamecock and I brought back from the Labyrinth. Don't forget—"

"There is no Dark One!"

A shout of elation, the response rolled back: "There is no Dark One!"

Theseus lifted the Falling Star. "You were slaves, and now you are free. But your freedom is still in danger. Because you have other masters—other enemies. Remember—their only power is the lie of the Dark One!

"Minos will come against us, now, with his hired Etruscan killers. He will attack us, with all the tricks of his lying wizardry. But there is no Dark One—that is the truth that will destroy the warlocks.

"Now patch up your wounds. Strike off your fetters. Arm yourselves, from the men we have slain. But don't forget that your best weapon is that one truth—there is no Dark One!"

A chant of victory rolled up into the smoky night: "There is no Dark One!"

Theseus stepped down from the pile of wood beside the screaming urn, and Cyron caught his arm. Hoarse from shouting in the battle, the pirate's voice was strained with new apprehension.

"Captain Firebrand!" he gasped. "The flames must have

122

warned the warlocks! For the scouts we sent are already back. They say that the Etruscans are already marching here from Knossos—four hundred strong—to wipe us out!"

TWENTY

"AND THE ETRUSCANS," Cyron went on anxiously, "can't be defeated by the simple truth that there is no Dark One. They fight for hire, and Minos lets them practice their own grim worship, without regard for the Dark One."

The keen eyes of Theseus swept the high palisade, the red coal beds where the barracks had been, the huddled battle-weary mutineers. His bare shoulders drew straight, and his hand went hard on the Falling Star.

"If the Etruscans fight for hire," he said, "they will fight for us when we have taken the treasury of Knossos."

Cyron stared and grunted doubtfully.

"A hundred men," Theseus told him, "can hold the palisade until the dawn, even against a thousand. I am going to leave you to hold it. I'll take sixty men and slip past the Etruscans and storm the palace tonight."

"Tonight?" breathed Cyron.

"Crete had three gods," rang the low voice of Theseus. "One of them still stands against us. Minos must die—tonight!"

Cyron studied his face in the fire glow and looked uneasily toward Knossos. "A hundred men," he said, "could hold the compound—against the Etruscans. But Minos may send lightning to fire the walls! Or the brass man to break them down!"

"You needn't fear that," Theseus promised him grimly. "I'll keep Minos and all his wizardry busy at Knossos."

But the hairy pirate caught his arm again. "I wish you wouldn't leave me, Captain Firebrand." His voice was unsteady, choked. "We have been comrades in many dangers." He gulped. "Let . . . let us take all who will follow and fight our way to the harbor town. We can be at sea by dawn, in the best galleys of Crete!"

"You shall have them, Gamecock—when we have taken Knossos," promised Theseus. "Now I am going to call for sixty willing men, to loot Knossos and end the domination of wizardry."

He climbed back to the pile of wood, and called for the volunteers, and waited. But none came forward.

"We can fight men," muttered the one-eyed Tirynthian cook. "But you ask us to make war on wizards and gods and a giant of brass!"

The Falling Star burned red in the fire glow.

"And they can be destroyed!" shouted Theseus. "The Dark One was the greatest god of Crete—and the Dark One was a lie! Blind fear is the sword and the yoke of wizardry—and it is fear of tricks and lies!

"Follow me—and remember there is no Dark One! The warlocks and the gods will fall before us. Even the brass man cannot stand against that truth. Now, who will come with me to claim the loot of Knossos?"

After a little uneasy pause, the one-eyed Tirynthian cook limped forward alone. "I'll go with you, Captain Firebrand," gasped Vorkos. "We must destroy the warlocks, as you say— or we shall be destroyed."

Theseus pointed at the tall black urn. "It is a law of Minos," he said, "that slaves who kill their masters shall die by slow torture. The pot is silent now. We must kill Minos tonight!"

That grim reasoning brought forward a steady trickle of men. Most of the surviving pirates came, and even a few of the former guards. Half a score of the blond Northern slave girls joined them. At first Theseus thought to stop the women. But when he saw the look upon their faces, and the way they carried their well-stained weapons, he let them come.

When the sixty were gathered, he led them to the gate, and turned back to promise Cyron: "When you see flames above Knossos, you can tell the hired Etruscans that their wages are stopped!"

The bearded Dorian came, blinking and blowing his nose, to embrace him. Then the tall gate creaked shut behind them. Theseus led the sixty in single file down a dry moonlit ravine toward the Kairatos River.

They lay hidden in black pools of shadow while the torches of the Etruscans marched along a hill above them. Then, silently—as the pirates had learned to march in a hundred midnight raids—they moved on through sleeping fields and dark groves and shadow-clotted vineyards.

One of the Cretan guards—who had joined them because Amur had given a girl slave whom he loved to the Minoan priests—silenced the barking dogs with his bow. There was no alarm, and at last the looming bulk of Knossos rose against the moonlit sky before them.

The palace was not a fortress. The first of its fabled walls was the fleet in the harbor, three miles away. The second was brazen Talos, whom they had not seen. The third—if Theseus could believe Ariadne—was the little talisman that he wore at his throat.

He had studied the tiny object, that afternoon. To the eye it was no more than a common seal cylinder, cut of dead-black steatite, pierced lengthwise. Its design, engraved with an exquisite perfection, showed a bull-headed giant, seated on a throne, with men and women kneeling.

Was this, really, the wall of wizardry? His mind had dwelt upon the riddle. Had Ariadne told the truth about its power? Could it really give him Knossos? If the Dark One himself did not exist, what power could lie in a mere picture?

The green-eyed loveliness of Ariadne had haunted Theseus, through all the dark passages of the Labyrinth. He couldn't make up his mind about her. She had been a scornful enemy —yet she had risked much to give him the Falling Star, so had saved his life.

Vessel of Cybele, she should know the illusion of love. In her thousand years or so, she must have loved too many men for any one to matter greatly. She was a member of the strange pantheon of Crete, and she knew that he planned to shatter her world. It was sheerest madness, he knew, to hope for any aid from her.

Yet the talisman was hanging at his throat, and her red-haired loveliness was smiling at him. Something mocked him, from her smile. Theseus tried to thrust it from his mind, and whispered to his sixty in the shadow of Knossos:

"We must destroy Minos, all his priests and warlocks, and the giant of brass. Daedalus must die—he is the most terrible wizard! But spare the slaves, the artisans, and all the common people—set them free with the word that there is no Dark One!"

125

"Aye, Captain Firebrand," whispered the one-eyed Tirynthian.

"There are two others you must spare," ordered Theseus. "One of them is Ariadne, the daughter of Minos, who is the vessel of Cybele—she gave me the Falling Star, to slay the Dark One.

"The other to be saved—if we happen to find him—is a small Babylonian wizard, called Snish, the cobbler—because he is my friend."

The pirates were well versed in the methods of raids by night. The sixty came up the hill as silently as shadows, and reached the artisan's entrance. There was a short, savage battle with the Etruscans in the wardroom, but the most of them died before they were fully awake. Snatching new arms from the arsenal there, the sixty fought their way into the corridors beyond.

"There is no Dark One!" The battle cry pealed through the ancient halls. "Theseus, the Firebrand, destroyed him! Join us, to take the loot of Knossos! For the gods are doomed!"

Bewildered men and women swarmed excitedly out into the halls and fled again. A few of the palace artisans came to join Theseus, but most of them were too startled to do anything at all. Sleepy, swearing Etruscan soldiers and black lancer-priests gathered hastily at points of vantage ahead.

Five stories high and six acres in extent, with its maze of courts and light wells and corridors and stairs and magazines, a thousand years in the building, Knossos was itself a second Labyrinth, as confusing as the limestone galleries of the Dark One's cavern temple.

Theseus himself was lost. But the artisans, and a slave who had served in the imperial household, pointed out the way toward the apartments of Minos. The sixty crushed through the stubborn groups of priests and Etruscans, fighting toward it.

The quick success of the raid began to seem slightly ominous to Theseus. His men met no barriers of wizardry, caught no glimpse of brazen Talos. And they pushed through to the megaron of Minos.

The Etruscans had gathered at the entrance for a final desperate stand. But elation of victory had turned the Falling Star to a darting flame of death, and the pirates followed it as they had done in a hundred other fights. The last Etruscan fell, and Theseus led his band through the splendid frescoed hall and into the bedchamber of Minos.

The startled ruler sat up on his magnificent canopied couch. Trembling and pale, his fat hands dragged the fine Egyptian linen up about his pink fat body, as if it could shield him from the dripping sword of Theseus.

The round baby-face had turned pale as the clutching hands, and it was not dimpled now. The little blue eyes had lost their merry twinkle, and terror glazed them. Thin and shuddering, the woman-voice shrilled:

"Spare me, Captain Firebrand! Spare my life, and all I have is yours to take. My treasury, my fleet, my empire! Only spare my life!"

Theseus held his lifted sword. He had come to kill a warlock. Here was only a fat old man, quaking with fear. Anger crackled in his voice: "Find a weapon! Fight for your throne!"

But Minos had gone speechless. A gross mass of pink flesh, he tumbled out of bed and sprawled, quivering and gasping, on the rugs. The light of the torches flickered over him. Theseus still withheld the sword.

"So this is the god Minos?" Scorn choked him. "The warlock who has reigned a thousand years, whose double ax is feared in Egypt and Cathay!" The Falling Star trembled in his hand. "I came here to kill you, Minos—to end the reign of wizardry. But I have never struck a kneeling, weeping man—"

"But I have, Captain Firebrand!" Vorkos, the one-eyed Tirynthian, strode forward. "Lend me your blade!"

He snatched the Falling Star. The bright steel hissed down. Severed cleanly, the white head of Minos rolled away from the gross quaking body, stared up mutely.

Head and body changed!

The Tirynthian dropped the Falling Star, staggered backward. Muttering fearfully, the pirates began to retreat toward the door. Theseus picked up the sword. He snatched a torch from a shuddering hand and bent to examine the thing that had been Minos.

Body and head were yellowed, waxen-pale, shrunk almost to naked bones. The body had been nearly bloodless—only a few black drops spilled from the severed arteries and veins. Only sorcery, Theseus knew, could have kept life in such a frame.

And the corpse—most incredible thing—was a woman's!

127

Theseus strove to put down the crawling fear that hideous sight had set in him. He tried to hold the steel blade steady in his hand, gulped vainly at the dry hoarseness in his throat.

"See!" he croaked at his apprehensive followers. "Minos is dead!" He pointed with the black-dripping blade, and it trembled. "And he was no god. He wasn't even a man. He was only an old, old woman!"

He moved with the torch toward the door. "We have conquered the gods of Crete!" He licked at his dry lips and tried again to swallow that hoarseness. "We have earned the loot of Knossos!"

"No, Captain Firebrand." The voice of the one-eyed cook was a rasp of dread. "The victory isn't won! For there is still the giant of brass, whose great feet can tramp us like vermin. There is still the wizard Daedalus, whose very glance can poison men. And still the daughter of Minos, who is a goddess and a sorceress."

Theseus dragged his eyes away from the shriveled, yellowed thing that had been Minos. "Ariadne is my friend—my lover," his dry whisper rasped. "Once she saved my life. Now we must find her—for her sorcery can aid us against the brass man and the wizard Daedalus."

He wiped the Falling Star and led his apprehensive band out of the splendid bedchamber of Minos. Dripping the scant black drops, the withered yellow body of the old, old woman lay still on the floor behind them.

TWENTY-ONE

OUT IN the planless maze of piled-up rooms and halls and stairs, where one chamber might be two steps above another, or three below, Theseus seized the dusty black pigtails of a palace stonecutter, who had joined them, and menaced him with the Falling Star, demanding:

"Where are the chambers of Ariadne?"

The frightened artisan shuddered, promised voicelessly to show the way.

All the palace was buzzing now, a disturbed human hive. Lamps and torches flared down dusky corridors. Men and women and children, slaves and free artisans who dwelt and labored in the vast pile, were screaming, running everywhere. Theseus and his men came upon a dozen more Minoan priests striving to barricade a passage, and fought again.

The steel sword led the pirates through the barrier, and every lancer died. But a coldness of dread was creeping up the spine of Theseus. It seemed to him again that success had been too easy.

Something was queerly wrong. A dozen riddles haunted him. Why had they met so few armed men—unless the palace was a trap? Where was Talos? What stand would Ariadne take? And what could he expect of the wall of wizardry? Why—most ghastly puzzle of all!—had Minos changed so strangely after he was dead?

The stonecutter led them to the spacious rich apartments of Ariadne. A sound of weeping met them, and they came upon a dozen red-clad temple girls. They were armed with bows and daggers, but they made no fight.

Theseus burst past them into the bedchamber. He tore aside the curtains, ripped the silken cover from the couch, flung open a great painted coffer, peered into the bath beyond. Ariadne was gone.

He seized one of the weeping girls by her scented hair, brushed her throat with the tip of the Falling Star, and asked the whereabouts of her mistress. The girl was speechless with fear.

"The goddess is gone!" she whispered at last. "She has fled —we don't know where!"

Theseus released the girl, stood baffled.

"Captain Firebrand!" That thin nasal croak was familiar. Theseus turned swiftly toward the doorway, found the squat form of Snish. The little Babylonian's yellow eyes were popping out with apprehension; teeth chattered in his huge mouth. "Captain Firebrand!"

"Snish—my friend!" Theseus greeted him with a relieved grin. "You've nothing to fear—my men have orders not to harm you. You're all right? How did you escape, that night at the grove?"

The little wizard waddled toward him, eagerly. "One of Ariadne's temple girls took a liking to me," he wheezed, "and kept me hidden." His enormous smirk showed huge yellow teeth. "Within limits, my small arts are useful in love!" The nasal voice sank. "Master, I have brought you a message from the goddess herself."

Theseus felt a little eager shudder. "From Ariadne?" He stepped closer to Snish. "What is the message?"

The voice of Snish became a nasal whisper: "She is waiting in a tower on the roof. She begs you to come to her. I'll show you the way. You must leave your men behind."

For an instant Theseus stood still, weighing the Falling Star in his hands. He listened to the increasing ominous humming that filled the palace, looked from his grim, red-stained followers back to the pop-eyed frog face of Snish.

Decision steadied the sword. "Wait for me," he told the one-eyed cook. "But, if I have not returned in the time it would take a bard to sing the battle song of Tiryns, take what loot you can carry and rejoin Cyron."

"Aye, Captain," muttered Vorkos. "But beware these warlocks!"

Turning to follow Snish: "Hasten!" whispered Theseus.

Waddling swiftly, the little wizard led him through a net of corridors and stairs and connected rooms so intricate that Theseus lost sense of direction. At last, pressing open a door where no joint had been visible, Snish led the way up a dark winding flight.

Abruptly, at that hidden door, all the humming confusion of the alarmed palace was left behind. There was no sound on that black stone stair—but the very silence was tense, menacing.

Theseus held the torch high with one hand and clutched his naked sword with the other. His companions, he knew, could never follow him here. He was alone. His blade touched the puffing little wizard.

"If this is betrayal, Snish," he rasped the warning, "you shall be the first to die!"

The little Babylonian looked back against the torchlight, his seamed brown face both aggrieved and frightened.

"Master!" His nasal voice quivered huskily. "When I have risked my life to bring this message, can't you trust me?" He shuddered to a long noisy sob, blew his nose. "Haven't I proved myself? Haven't I saved your life a dozen times?"

"Perhaps," said Theseus. "Lead on—swiftly. I have warned you!"

130

The dark stair brought them up, at last, through the floor of a huge dim room. Dust set Snish to coughing, and the flaring torch cast eerie shadows into cobwebbed corners. Theseus peered hastily about, wondering.

The lofty walls were covered with racks of sealed, labeled jars that held papyrus scrolls. Stacked clay tablets made brown mountains. Long shelves were covered with odd-shaped vessels of metal, pottery, and glass. Sturdy, blackened benches bore implements of glass and polished metal, such as Theseus had never seen.

Perched upon a great, polished silver ball, that rose above a confusion of twisted black rods, gleaming copper wires and shimmering mirrors, was a huge black vulture. The bird's carrion reek filled the room. It moved a bald red head, following them with a flaming, malignant black eye.

Theseus set the trembling point of his sword against the back of Snish. "Wait!" he gasped. "What place is this?"

There was something curiously froglike in the little wizard's startled jump.

"This is the workshop of Daedalus, called the artificer," he croaked. "But trust me, master—and put away your sword!" His popping yellow eyes blinked earnestly. "Truly, I am guiding you to the goddess. There is only one more flight to climb."

"Lead on," rapped Theseus. "But if we meet the warlock—he dies!"

The vulture made a raucous, startling scream, and the sinister eye followed them across the long dusty room. The torch found a narrow stair, and Snish led the way upward again. They came out upon a parapeted roof beneath the moon, and a gust of cold wind extinguished the burned-out torch.

Theseus stared ahead, speechless.

Before them, gleaming under the moon, was such a thing as he had never glimpsed or imagined. It was vaguely like a ship, for there were broad sails of white linen, and slender yards of polished wood, and rigging of thin, bright wire. But the sails lay horizontal. The thing rested upon flimsy-seeming wheels. There was no proper hull, but only a tiny cabin, in the midst of the spidery web of wood and cloth and metal. A door opened in that cabin.

"Captain Firebrand!"

It was the voice of Ariadne, strong and golden, yet with a husky little catch in it.

"You came—I knew you would!"

She climbed down flimsy steps. The full moon caught the red waves of her hair, strong enough to show color. Her white body was tall and sinuous as ever, intoxicating in a low-cut gown of clinging green. The serpent girdle writhed about her slender waist, and the ruby eyes glittered balefully.

She came swiftly to Theseus. Smooth bare arms slipped about him, drew him to her. Her face lifted, white and alluring under the moon. Theseus kissed her—but he kept a firm grip on the hilt of the Falling Star.

Her clinging lips drew reluctantly away from his. She caught his tense sword arm, drew him toward that fantastic, unsubstantial construction.

"I'm so glad, Captain!" Her voice throbbed huskily. "I have waited for you—and for Keke, my poor white dove, that was frightened by the fighting and flew away. But I'll leave Keke."

Her persuasive vibrant arm slipped around him again. "I knew that you would come to me, when your work in Crete was done. Because you promised. And I am ready, Captain. We'll be in Egypt before dawn!"

Theseus held back. "What is this thing?"

"This is the most wonderful fruit of all the wizardry of Crete," she told him. "It is a machine, that flies like a bird. Daedalus built it—and it is safer than the first, fragile machine, that killed his son. It is moved with an engine of fire, and it can lift us safely over the sea to Egypt, as fast as a vulture flies."

Her warm arm tugged again. "Come, my captain!"

"But why must we go to Egypt?" demanded Theseus. "To-night?"

"Don't you see?" Her golden voice was muted, pleading, anxious. "It is because of what you have done. You have destroyed the Dark One. You have slain Minos. You have raised the people, against all the warlocks and the gods."

Her warm body shuddered against him, and he felt the cold, writhing stiffness of the silver serpent.

"Don't you see?" She clung to him. "I must go, to save my life. The people would burn me in the temple of Cybele." Her tremulous lips kissed him. "But I waited for you, Captain."

Theseus crushed her tall, slim body against him, kissed her until they both were breathless. But he was watching Snish, over her shoulder, and he kept a good grasp on the Falling Star.

"Come on, my captain," she begged huskily. "The machine is loaded with my jewels and all the silver it can carry. If you aren't happy in Egypt, we can fly on, beyond, even to the edge of the world."

But Theseus waited, watchfully. "I'm not sure," he whispered, "that my task in Crete is done."

Her tall body tensed against him, and: "You have killed Minos," she protested quickly. "You have roused the people against the wizards and broken the power of the Dark One. What else have you to do?"

Theseus watched a white dove that came fluttering up out of the dark stairwell. It alighted on Ariadne's perfumed hair. She lifted a white hand, brought it down to her lips, kissed its beak.

"My little darling Keke!" she whispered. "My poor white dove. Was it lost? Is it afraid? Does it want to fly with us, on the wizard's wings, to Egypt?"

Cooing softly, the dove fluttered back to her shoulder. It cocked its head, and a bright eye looked at Theseus. That eye glittered under the moon. There was something familiar in its bright blackness, something—dreadful!

Ariadne reached for the hand of Theseus.

"Now, Captain," her golden voice rang eagerly, "Keke has come back. Let's go—before the people storm the tower or fire it."

But Theseus had stepped swiftly back. The Falling Star was ready in his hand. As if itself alive, the steel blade flashed up through the moonlight, slashed off the head of the cooing dove.

The bird fell from the bare white shoulder of Ariadne. It fluttered on the roof and lay still. Her golden voice went sharp, in a cry of grief and anger.

"What have you done?" She sobbed. "My beautiful Keke!"

But Theseus stood back from her, alertly watching the white headless bird. He saw it swell under the moon, and change. It became a man's body, nude, dark, gnarled, hairy, shriveled with years. It was headless, like the bird, and thick black blood spurted from the severed neck.

Theseus found the shaggy black head, lying beyond the feet of Ariadne. He turned it over with his toe, so that he could see the face. Snarling up at him, hideous in death, he saw the dark, skeletal visage of Daedalus.

White and motionless, Ariadne made a small choked sound.

"No, I'm not ready to go with you to Egypt," Theseus told her in a slow, grave voice. "I believe that I have another task to do. If you wish to wait, I'll come back to you when it is done."

He turned to Snish.

"Come with me again," he told the popeyed, shuddering little wizard. "Find me the brass man, Talos. I want to see what he looks like—dead!"

The white features of Ariadne stiffened again with terror. Her mouth half opened. Her hands lifted in a frantic gesture toward her throat. Then it seemed that something paralyzed her. Her scream was stifled.

"I'll wait," she whispered.

And Theseus followed the quaking little wizard down the stair.

TWENTY-TWO

THESEUS WALKED close at the heels of Snish, down into the black, dusty workroom of the dead warlock. The trembling yellow wizard lit a new torch from a dimly glowing brazier, and Theseus saw that the black vulture was gone from its perch on the silver ball.

Snish was a sallow green with fear, and the torch fell out of his quivering fingers. Theseus picked it up and followed him down that narrow winding stair into the ancient pile of Knossos. He could hear the frightened clatter of the wizard's teeth.

"Once, in Babylon," came the sobbing nasal wheeze of Snish, "I was an honest cobbler. I had a wife who was faithful except when she was drunk—and that was seldom, for we were very poor."

He stumbled on the narrow stone steps, caught himself.

"Knossos will kill me yet!" he gasped apprehensively. "And I was happy in Babylon—if I had only known it—until that magician brought me his boots to mend. I wish that I had never heard of wizardry!"

He paused on a narrow landing, and his huge yellow eyes blinked fearfully against the torch.

"Master," he croaked hollowly, "have you thought what you are doing? This brazen man has no humanity. He knows no pity. He may squeeze the life out of me, for letting you disturb his slumber. And he'll surely destroy you, Captain Firebrand. In a thousand years, he has not been vanquished."

His trembling hands made an urgent gesture. "Why don't you forget this folly, master?" he wheezed uneasily. "Why leave your bones to rot in the pits of Knossos—when there is a goddess waiting for you?"

Theseus came up to him, clutching torch and sword. "I came to Crete to do a task." His voice rapped hard. "It isn't done. Lead on."

With shuffling, uncertain steps, Snish guided him ahead. It began to seem a little ominous to Theseus that they came to no open court or shaft, saw no light burning, found no human being. Only once, for a moment, did they hear any sound —distant shouting and the far-off clash of arms.

"What is that?" demanded Theseus.

Snish paused and turned to listen, and it seemed to Theseus that his bulging yellow eyes were staring through the damp black walls. His huge bald head nodded slowly.

"That is your comrade, Cyron the Gamecock," he said. "He has come to join your men, and they are hunting the last of the Minoan priests to their lairs. This night is indeed the end of wizardry in Crete!"

"Cyron?" Theseus stared doubtfully at Snish. "But I left him to hold the compound!"

Snish listened again, at the niter-crusted wall.

"The Gamecock is telling your one-eyed cook what happened. He left three women to tend the watch fires in the palisade, and laid an ambush for the Etruscans on the road from Ekoros. He convinced them that the people had risen against them. They took the compound and fortified themselves to wait for day."

"Good old Gamecock!" Theseus grinned, returned to frowning soberness. "Lead on, wizard."

He followed Snish, and the dim sounds faded. They de-

135

scended into a dank, brooding stillness that Theseus well knew, from the time he had been in the dungeon. It was the silence and the fetor of death.

Following on closely, Theseus coughed from the acrid sting of decay in the air. He started to the dull, hollow echo of their footsteps. Suddenly it seemed to him that Snish, for a stranger newly come from Babylon, was ominously familiar with this dark labyrinth. He hung back, at a long hall's entrance.

"Where are you taking me?" Apprehension croaked in his own throat. "Where is Talos?"

Snish pointed down the black-pillared hall.

"We can wait here, master." His huge yellow eyes rolled uneasily, and his voice was a rasping whisper. "If you still seek to die. For Talos will come this way."

Theseus looked anxiously down the lofty avenue of square black columns, but nothing moved among them. He listened, and heard only the hissing crackle of the torch and his own hastening heart.

"We'll wait," he said. "But how do you know that Talos will come?"

The yellow eyes of Snish blinked at him, gravely. "I'm a wizard," wheezed the squat Babylonian, "if only a very minor one." He came waddling back to Theseus, his ugly, wide-mouthed face pale and tense in the torchlight. "I know another small device, master," he wheezed, "that can serve when Talos comes!"

Theseus stepped back, watchfully. "What is that?"

Snish reached out a quivering hand. "Give me your sword, master," came his nasal rasp. "My insignificant arts can make it invisible, so that you will seem to stand facing Talos with empty hands. That small advantage might well decide the fight."

But Theseus held the sword, set its bright point against the wizard's middle.

"The Falling Star has served me well," he rapped. "And it will again—as it is!"

The yellow flame of the torch flared brighter in the yellow eyes of Snish. They seemed to expand. Their glare, for a moment, was almost terrible. They reminded Theseus— But Snish was abruptly shivering and breathless.

"M-m-m-master!" he stammered faintly. "It's T-T-T-Talos!" His quivering yellow arm pointed past Theseus, down the brooding hush of the black colonnade. "The b-b-b-brass man, coming—"

Gripping the sword, Theseus crouched and turned. There was only darkness between the rows of columns. He moved the torch, and silent, monstrous shadows leaped among them. But there was no gleam of brass, nor any tread of metal feet. Swiftly, he turned again.

Snish was gone. Where he had been, stood—Talos!

The brazen giant was bending. The torchlight shone on his bright, flexing skin, and his flaming eyes were huge yellow lamps. Splendid muscles bulged his colossal body, and tendons thrummed like lyre strings. The fist of Talos, knotted into a huge brazen mace, was descending in a swift and deadly blow.

Theseus ducked. He swung the Falling Star, putting all his strength into a swift, instinctive thrust. The mighty fist slipped past his shoulder. And the steel nicked the mighty beam of the giant's forearm.

Theseus leaped back. "*You*—" he whispered. "Talos!"

His prompt defense had been all automatic. Now belated terror toppled upon him like a falling wall. Cold sweat covered him, and his quivering hand loosened on the Falling Star.

Talos crouched lower, uttering a tremendous brazen cry of pain and rage. It was like the bellow of some monstrous beast. Slow drops of liquid flame dripped from the slashed waist. They spattered into little blazing pools on the stone floor.

"Well, Captain Firebrand!" The sudden laughter of Talos was deafening thunder in the long hall, and his yellow-flaming eyes were brighter than the torch. "If you could see the look on your face!"

Both gleaming fists balled, he stalked upon Theseus.

"Talos, you see, was no fool, after all!" boomed that terrible voice. "For he was also the little Babylonian cobbler, who was always aiding you, Captain—to reach this moment of your destined death."

The numbed brain of Theseus was groping back. The fearful little wizard, he realized, had always contrived to slip away just before Talos appeared.

The giant laughed again. "Snish came to aid you," rolled the voice of Talos, "because it was written in the screed of

137

time that a red-haired Greek should win in the games, and vanquish the Dark One, and slay Minos—and written also that then the wizardry of Knossos should prevail again!"

Talos crouched lower.

"With the aid of Snish, all the destined events took place with the minimum of harm. When they had taken place, we had hoped for you to leave Crete, with the daughter of Minos —who offered to give herself up to you, for her father's sake. But you refused to go, and now your time has come to die!"

He brandished a mighty metal fist, and a drop of flame from his bleeding arm splashed the thigh of Theseus. He flinched, and the brass giant laughed again.

"Now, do you think that Talos was the fool?" The great voice rolled and reverberated among the massive black columns. "Or were you? Snish guided you past the wooden wall, and past the wall of brass. But, mortal, there is still the wall of wizardry. While it stands, Knossos cannot fall. Think of that—and die!" Bellowing like a brazen bull, Talos lumbered forward.

Theseus still shuddered from the shock of fear. The treachery of Snish had not completely surprised him, for he had clung to a resolve to trust no wizard. Yet it seemed to him now that he had let himself be guided to the door of final defeat.

He had accomplished nothing real. All his seeming victories had been no more than the moves of a toy man, in a game of the gods of Knossos. He was certain now, that the old woman had not been Minos. Talos, he thought, would surely kill him now. And the reign of wizardry would continue, as if he had never striven to end it.

Theseus leaped aside from the ponderous rush of Talos, and his eyes flashed down at the little black seal cylinder, hung by the thin silver chain at his throat. If Ariadne had promised him that wizardry could not prevail against the holder of the talisman, she had warned him, too, not to trust its efficacy.

Talos saw his glance, paused to laugh and roar a mocking question: "Mortal, was Talos the fool?"

No, Theseus thought, he himself had been, for Ariadne was a goddess of Crete. Her kisses must have been just one more move in the game. So must have been her gift of the black seal cylinder—and her lie that it was the wall of wizardry. Even her action in giving him the Falling Star when he went into the Labyrinth, he saw now, had only served to bring him here, face to face with Talos and death.

Ariadne, he bitterly perceived, had proved herself false. Mistress of wizardry herself, she had surely known that Snish was also Talos—yet had let him follow the little magician here, unwarned. Anyhow, Theseus told himself, woman or witch, her kisses had been sweet!

Talos rushed again, and Theseus struck with the Falling Star. The steel blade slashed a mighty fist; drops of liquid fire oozed from bright metal. The furious bellow of Talos shook the columns and dislodged a shower of plaster fragments. He charged again.

Again Theseus leaped aside, beneath the flashing sword. The great fist just grazed his shoulder. But still the force of it staggered him, its heat blistered his skin. He stumbled back, wiping sweat out of his eyes.

The battle, he saw, could have only one ending.

His thrusts were merely painful. They inspired a certain brief caution in Talos, and won him a few more breaths of life. But he could hope to inflict no mortal wound. Already he was tiring, staggering. And mounting rage was swiftly overwhelming the brass man's caution.

Once his eyes flicked about, in desperate hope of aid or escape. But there was small possibility that his men could find him here—or aid him if they did. And Talos, huge yellow eyes blazing cunningly, kept between him and the entrance. He was helplessly trapped.

Theseus tried to side-step the next flailing blow. But, drugged with weariness and dread, he moved too slowly. The searing edge of the tremendous fist just touched his temple— and sent him spinning, to fall against the base of a square black column.

Red pain obscured his vision. His breath was gone. Struggling to drag himself upright, he found that the Falling Star was lost. He blinked his dimming eyes and saw the great foot of Talos come down upon the sword.

Hot brass hands reached down for the body of Theseus. He looked into the flaming eyes beyond them, and saw fearful, unexpected depths of rage and hate, and knew that those hands would twist his body like a rag, wringing out viscera and blood. But still he couldn't rise.

"Captain Firebrand!"

His ringing ears heard that urgent golden voice, and his

139

clearing eyes saw Ariadne. She stood at the black hall's entrance, behind the brazen giant. The torch she carried flamed red against her hair, and green in her eyes, and white on her heaving breast.

"Captain—I lied to you!" Agony choked her. "Break the wall of wizardry!"

The bellow of Talos was raucously deafening. Frightful rage twisted the metal face, and hate flamed hideous in the yellow eyes. The giant dropped on his knees, and both gigantic fists came crushing down.

Theseus knew that he must obey Ariadne—if he had time! He snatched the little black cylinder, snapped the silver chain. Frantically his eyes searched for anything he could use for a hammer, to shatter it. But Talos knelt upon the sword, and there was nothing he could reach.

"Break it!" Ariadne was sobbing. "Do not fear for me. I have saved the secrets of my own essential science. Break it—now!"

Desperately, Theseus twisted at the talisman with his fingers. The hard black stone abruptly crumbled, as if turned to friable clay. It crushed into dust.

Talos stiffened, the great fists suspended.

Theseus heard a tremendous rumbling—like the bellow of some unimaginably monstrous bull, he thought, lost in some ultimate cavern. The floor pitched sharply.

"My daughter—" The great voice of Talos quavered queerly, a dying gong. "Why—"

The brass giant was tossed back across the heaving floor. Staggering, he struck a great square column. It buckled. Huge black stones came toppling down. The squared capital, which must have weighed many tons, caught Talos on the shoulders.

Theseus seized his torch and the Falling Star. He came swaying to his feet. The floor still bucked like a deck in a storm. Dust choked him. Walls were crashing everywhere, and that tortured bull still bellowed underground.

Gripping the sword, he lunged toward the brass man. But Talos, pinned beneath the fallen capital, was already dead—and changing!

The head protruding from below that immense black stone had become human again. But it was not the head of Snish. The face was round and pink and dimpled, crowned with fine white hair. The small blue eyes, even as they glazed, seemed

140

to twinkle against the torchlight in a ghastly mockery of merriment.

"Minos!"

Theseus stumbled back, the torch trembling in his cold hands.

"Then what—what was the other? That old, old woman?"

Ariadne came slowly through the raining debris to his side. Though her cool green eyes were dry, she shook with stifled sobs. Quivering, she clung to him. As the bellowing in the earth sank away, he could hear her stricken voice.

"She was my mother. This—this was my father."

Theseus kissed her dusty forehead, and turned her away, and led her through the hail of plaster and broken stone out into the long central court. A lurid yellow pillar stood roaring in the night above shattered Knossos, for the long west wing was already burning.

Shuddering suddenly, Ariadne clung to Theseus.

"What's happening?" he whispered. "What caused all this?"

"The wall of wizardry was a strong spell." She paused to sob, but then her voice was queerly calm. "It had guarded Knossos and my father from all harm, for many hundred years. It had been a dam against the stream of time. It had stopped needful change. Strains had grown against it, in the facts of history and in the very rocks beneath. The suspended laws of chance were waiting for revenge. When you broke the dam, you loosed the force of pent-up centuries—against my father's throne!"

He peered at her, puzzled.

"Against yourself, too?"

"What do you think?" Her warm arms clung to him. Winking away her tears, she lifted her face. Beneath the blaze of burning Knossos, she remained white and young and lovely.

He shook his head uncertainly.

"Don't you like my new sort of science?" Beneath the dying bellow of the earth and the roaring storm of flame, her low laugh was melodious and faintly mocking. "You see, I have learned to apply the laws of nature in a slightly different way. My true science shall prevail, where all the old magic has failed."

Hesitant, he almost pushed her away.

"But I did it all for you, Captain Firebrand." Her golden voice sank huskily. "I had learned the new science from old

141

Daedalus, who dabbled in both kinds, but I broke the wall of wizardry for you. I should do it again. Because you have taught me that human truth is more splendid—more powerful—than all the tricks and illusions of magic. I renounce the power of wizardry—or almost all of it—for you."

Her serpent girdle was under the hand of Theseus. He felt it abruptly stiffen. Looking down, he saw that the malific glitter had gone from the ruby eyes. He caught the dead metal, straightened it, drew it away from her waist. Laying aside the Falling Star, he pulled her hard against him.

She kissed him bewitchingly.